Also available from

Denver Day:

Pizza Noir No. 2: "Alpha Taxonomy" (2015)

Pizza Noir No. 3: "Pie in the Sky" (2017)

Hipster Bricks: A Philosophical Novel (2016)

The Only Game in Town (coming in 2018)

PIZZA NOIR
1

PIZZA NOIR

#1

Catch as Catch Can

Denver Day

Fourth Edition
Day, Denver, author
Braswell, C.G., editor & publisher
Braswell Business Communications Services Inc., printer

Literature is art, all dharma is fire, this copy of *Pizza Noir No. 1 – Catch as Catch Can* is yours to keep.

Pizza Noir is a work of fiction cut from whole cloth. None of these events occurred nor do the characters exist although they easily could, probably might, and perhaps should, notwithstanding arguments from wardens and werewolves.

Rev. date: October 2025

To order additional copies of the book contact:
Braswell Business Communications Services Inc.
1-520-255-7193
www.fusepowder.com
www.denverday.com

contents

CHAPTER ONE: WHEN ARRIVENSATA
FRESH MURDER SCENE, POLICE ARE
SURPRESED TO FIND A COUPLE OF
STRIPPERS AND A DEAD PIZERIA DELIVERY
MAN WHO LEFT THE SCRASIN THE CAR.

Three Cold Ones

I'm going about my business on this given morning. Four in the morning. Coffee in the street, and it's foggy, wet and relatively quiet in these precious fleeting moments of municipal tranquility. Static as it may be now, the air's pregnant with anticipation of bustle, it is already conducting the approaching vibrations of car and people traffic.

"You know, this weather makes it easier to appreciate yer shitty coffee, Joey," I remarked to the vendor at the kiosk.

Joey has been selling me newspapers at State and Main for eighteen months. In my case, this man is selfless with his cheap, hot, brown water. He looked up into the fog and tapped out a short, filterless morning square.

"What a mess. No leads but the dead," he observed, picking up on our previous conversation.

"Mess is right," I said, but it's the kind of mess that gives me a challenge, and that is an upshot. A dead pizza delivery man, among a distribution of corpses without any obvious correlation but for the one, obvious one connection outside of happenstance. The girl, age 19, is a cliché-in-state; a suburban daughter -come-call girl, who'd gone to the big city and become forever lost. 'Til by death did she part as a victim from so many angles.

When found, her throat was slit and she lay dead a'floor next to two others. And the pizza man, an Asian male melted from the neck with some razor-sharp edge, was laying between the girl and a mysterious, picture-perfect Euro in a new suit who was likewise finely splayed. The pieman's name was Stephen Wang. His meat cake remained on the ground of the scene untouched and still warm in the box that took one good hop when its bereaved dropped it.

The suited man was evidently 19's customer; maybe she and the deliveryman were just on the wrong where-when. But I doubt it. All of it a sad transaction, but not of the sort that would typically marshal this particular brand of instant kharma.

A fact most likely useless beyond forensic trivia, is that the pizza man had forgotten the sodas in his car, according to the bloody bill of goods for the food delivery.

I looked up at the bottomless fog. It's not

dawn, but it would be hard to see the sun through the city's soup even if it were. I admit that I love this weather, muddy as it is. I passed my polystyrene cup, somewhat bigger than a shot glass, back to captain coffee for a refill.

I'm looking at my watch. I glance out the window, then back to my desk. It's ten past one. I spent all morning panning for investigative gold among the denizens of the down-town. The best lead that isn't a dead person is a tangent from the girl, the only surface to scratch so far. Luckily, I make my own hours.

These seedy cases involve people who dwell in a perpetual purgatory where lies are the best facts available, the wages of sin are highly competitive, and everything's pretty fuzzy. A sort of non-linear reality underneath the typical landscape of the day walkers among us. To make sense of it, you have to blend in and cast off moral crutches and lifelines in order to walk on your own in this very big gray area. Yet for all of that, in some ways, people, or perhaps just the human condition, seem the only non-variable.

So I "put the machine on it." The investigator's shovel, so to speak. I suppose every profession has its noted domain and implements. It's bracing, even exciting, to see what holds up to evaluation and what does not. Surprising too, sometimes, because you come to realize that everybody you deal with is "in character," and then you're the only one who's holding up the walls. Some even share the desire to remain alive and above room temperature, but that's about the end of the common ground.

Reverse-engineering the Asian pizza man came without the benefit of a liquored-up little league coach, but the dead girl wasn't as strings-free, as her sweet daddy was left alone on this green earth to discuss with me his daughter's dark and rueful demise. So meanwhile, right in front of me, he died some more on his insides, suffering through frantic denial regarding the fate of his estranged little girl.

The pizza man left behind a woman who argued that she, not the dropped pizza was his bereaved. His girlfriend I say, she identified herself as his fiance, but what's the difference. She was without an ounce of shame although she did have plenty of cocaine all over her face upon answering the door.

The pie-man's lover's voice sounded like a

helium-addled poodle high on crack with a burr in in its ass, in a corrugated-metal barn intentionally designed for enhanced echo, during a nighttime helter-skelter-nado. I speculate, the pizza man is better off dead than with this gal, if in fact he really was locked into anything permanent with her. They say family is forever.

Anyway, the woman hit on me when she opened the door. Keri Anders. She had liar and grifter tattooed on her forehead in big black glowing bright paisley spades. She had an unusually clear head for a tweaker.

(Heartland law enforcement professionals will tell you stories about finding extremely large, amazing collections of arrowheads in busted-up meth dens, collections gathered by sleepless tweakers with crank-induced, eagle-eye tunnel vision and enduring insomnia. They walk their local hills spotting these otherwise well camouflaged native implements with great ease.)

But her time would come, and a tweaker she clearly was, of the highest and most checkered and sundry stripe. Superhuman until she eventually burns up from the inside-out like a bale of speed-addled hay. I softshoed it, left her my card. The pharmaceutical plume hanging

Denver Day

inside Anders' apartment made me jittery, elevated my heart rate, and made me need to take a shit. It comes with the territory.

Thirdly; so far, that suit remains an anonymous pocketful of cash-sans-identification. Among trails like this, I bump into similar versions of countless others like him, anonymously darkening doors of the types of places where this nameless man's last act happened.

OK. Nachos, the last thing to pack, check. Flask of 'skey, check. Cannister of coffee, check. Short squares, check. Extra clips, check. Petrol, full, ready. A nice (again) moist, unassuming evening. Perfect. The usual, not cold, not hot; just soupy, just right, a slightly obscurely back-lit drizzle. My version of inland Atlantis. I watched the pizza widow catch a lift in a late-model, primer-painted sports sedan with t-tops about 10. The vehicle made directly to a nightclub in the central district.

I wrote down the plates and followed them to a sushi bar about ten minutes away. Shortly, this little caravan returned to the club. The driver reversed into the back parking lot and walked in the door with an armload of oriental takeout.

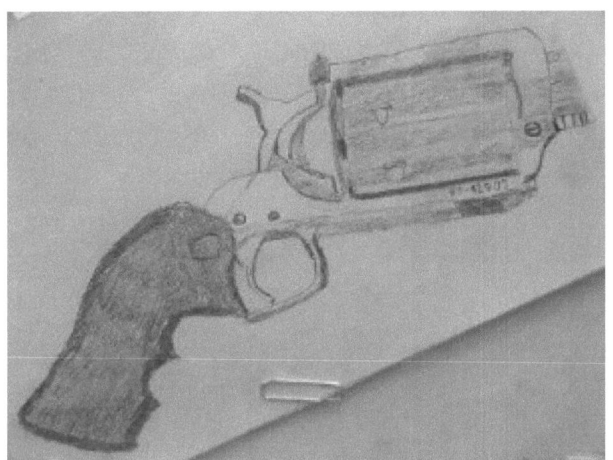

Clean Living and Rubber Gloves

I drove back around and parked by the front entrance, and did parking lot duty for about ninety minutes, making note of all the faces I saw come and go. I jotted down license plate numbers by the dashboard light. To see and be seen, every thirty minutes or so I strolled around the lot and had a smoke. But I can't just hang out in parking lots all night. It's not sociable.

On the side of the building, a doorman sat on a bar stool under the eave near the structure's northwest corner. He was not much more than a lit cigar, squared-away with a crew cut and a boxy brown coat, and the cover charge was a Jackson note. The place was a skin joint called the Diddler On The Roof, and it was crowded. Saturday.

It seemed less humid, or at least *different* humid on the inside; the thick smoke dried the air out, and the HVAC did something interesting with the building's dew point and temperature. It might also have to do with the source of the humidity, as from within there was a lot more evaporating sweat, alcohol, and other designer odors. Ahhh, summer nights.

There was an elaborate stripper pier occupying the relative center of the main room, with a trap-door egress whence the dancers would emerge, and hence performing their numbers withdraw again wither. There was a long, long, long bar across the north wall of the big room, occupied by a busy and accordingly sizable bar staff. My coat and shoes were black so my lightly worn baby face didn't stick out in the younger, hipper martini crowd.

I knew there was probably some whiskey back there to abide, somewhere; Time was pushing the witching hour, and I hailed one of the barkeeping staff, ordered a neat glass, and had her provide me with some petty cash on a bar tab. The entire ceiling was mirrored. The girls dancing on the stage, including the pie man's widow Anders, rotated through as the night proceeded. Her jig had tears, melodrama, allegorical projection, and all the fixin's to go along with it. Though very dark, it really made for an evocative artistic experience that was misunderstood by her audience and her.

An island, a beacon, she; what a rock. Some of the dancers, as had Ms. Anders when she answered my knock at her apartment, had failed to completely get all of the cocaine off of their faces and bodies before they emerged from the stage floor's trap door. Furthermore, despite the mirrors on the ceiling and the criminal codification of the substance, honking it right out loud was an ubiquitous act among the Diddler's patrons and staff.

Not that I'm one to criticize or judge; and I stopped paying attention to politics years ago when I quit the working press, but I would prefer swinging doors, a jukebox, wobbly and graffitied tables, and more nostalgic aromas which do not contain second hand crack cocaine smoke. In my convalescence, I am inclined toward more pastoral things from simpler times passed. You know it when you see it, but in retrospect, it's all the same anyway.

Granted, tonight is these people's night off, not mine. But all the yeo in the air gave me the jitters and made me have to take another shit. Again, the usual workplace hazards. I put a couple Jacksons in her holster, and gave her a smile. She gave me the crocodile eye.

By now, it was about 2:30 and the place was about to close for business when a crowded bang emerged from the west side of the room, chased by shattering glass and a bawling, brawling ball of about 20 people kicking the shit out of whoever had let loose into the ceiling mirror with their Roscoe. I took this opportunity to mosey around past that particular clusterfuck and back out to my car. I idled 'round to the back again, turned on some instant-classic amplitude modulation signals, and watched the foot traffic coming out of the backdoor.

Ms. Anders left with the dude who had brought the takeout dinner back-stage earlier that evening, but they only drove so far as the inn a half-block away.

It looked like most of the staff and many of the club patrons were headed to the same destination, and many of them just walked that short distance from the club. It must be a regular after-hours ritual in this neighborhood, I thought. The lobby of the roadhouse next door was crowded with blinking patrons whose eyes were adjusting to the relative light and quiet compared to that of the heavily black-lit nightclub scene.

There was a lounge on the north side of the ground floor, with a fully active bar offering additional darkness and humidity, into which the crowd was making its way. There was a lounge-jazz band playing steadily ahead into the wee three o'clock hour. Anders sat at a booth on the south side of the lounge, along with her incumbent driver (an Asian Chinese takeout man) and four other dudes I hadn't seen before.

One of those dudes broke out a big ball of Andes Mountains marching dust, and they all went to town with it right there at their booth table.

The smooth lounge jazz heated up slightly. I'm sure the hotel bar had whiskey, but I ordered a porter ale instead. I had a smoke with the sax player when the band took five, and I was pleased and refreshed to encounter the saxophonista.

She said the lounge getting busy after the

Denver Day

nightclub closed made for a regular cycle which translated into a very solid and steady gig for the band among other parties concerned. That is, good business for the club's working girls, she said, as well as the hotel's shareholders and the patrons, et al. Some were one in the same. The scene throbbed and pulsed like a black hole. I took her card, and told her I'd like to get a coffee with her sometime when I wasn't working.

The band went back to their work, and I to mine, following Ms. Anders and her five dates up the crowded stairs. She had noticed me in the lounge, and when she saw me on the stairs she invited me to join for an after-hours drink. The green-shag-carpeted suite was, itself, also crowded. Anders seemed the lady of the hour. I excused myself from the den and walked to the restroom to liberate bio-fluids internally displaced by the ale, all the while making note of the faces I was encountering in the suite.

As I emerged from the toilet, I looked over at the plush sofa and beheld Anders on her back with two of her dates under her, and two more guys on top of her, and several more fucking her head. She looked like a spider with each arm holding a different insect. From her crowded mouth came a sound like a bobcat in a wood chipper. While I was in the can, they had engineered and built a fleshy, closed-loop airlock system with spare plugs orbiting in the wait.

When I had walked out of my door that morning, I hadn't expected to see that many tattoos during the course of my regular business. Especially not all at the same time.

It was getting pretty early anyway. It looked like I'd have to wait until tomorrow for any further verbal conversation with Keri Anders. I zipped my coat and made for Joe's coffee stand.

"I guess the two main questions go like this: Number one, what's her deal with Chinese culinary professionals; and two, when are you going to arrest her?" Joe commented.

The air this 4 a.m. is much the same as yesterday and every other morning, with our proximity to the ocean to thank for the fidelity of this year-round pea soup, and I considered this, as well as the also-welcome predictability of Joe's dry wit and coffee. Truth be told, he was probably right.

"No shit that, Joe. No shit," I said. "The lieutenant and I will talk to her tomorrow. Playing devil's advocate, it could've been a random end-user burn on a drug deal. Or it could have been her new-new Asian delivery beau, with Anders as an accessory. Is the motive jealousy, or dope, or a combination of those. Wrap up the investigation from there. Then a judge for a warrant. Probably wind up in a plea bargain. We might need extra popcorn if it goes to trial, but I doubt that."

"Yep. Probably a big ol' pot of all-of-the-above gumbo. Airlock, huh. We used to call that a clusterfuck. Must be good pussy or good dope to drive those kids to blood like that," Joe editorialized over the coffee pot. He poured us each another polystyrene cupful.

"I'll stick to my stogies and cigarettes. Nobody's ever tried to fillet me over either one," he grinned. "Yet."

This from a guy who pours whiskey in his coffee before the sun's up.

"Yeh, Joe, just look at ya. Well, everyday is Halloween for some people," I offered. I finished my hot brown breakfast du Joe, and headed to my apartment, hitting the rack at the day's first light.

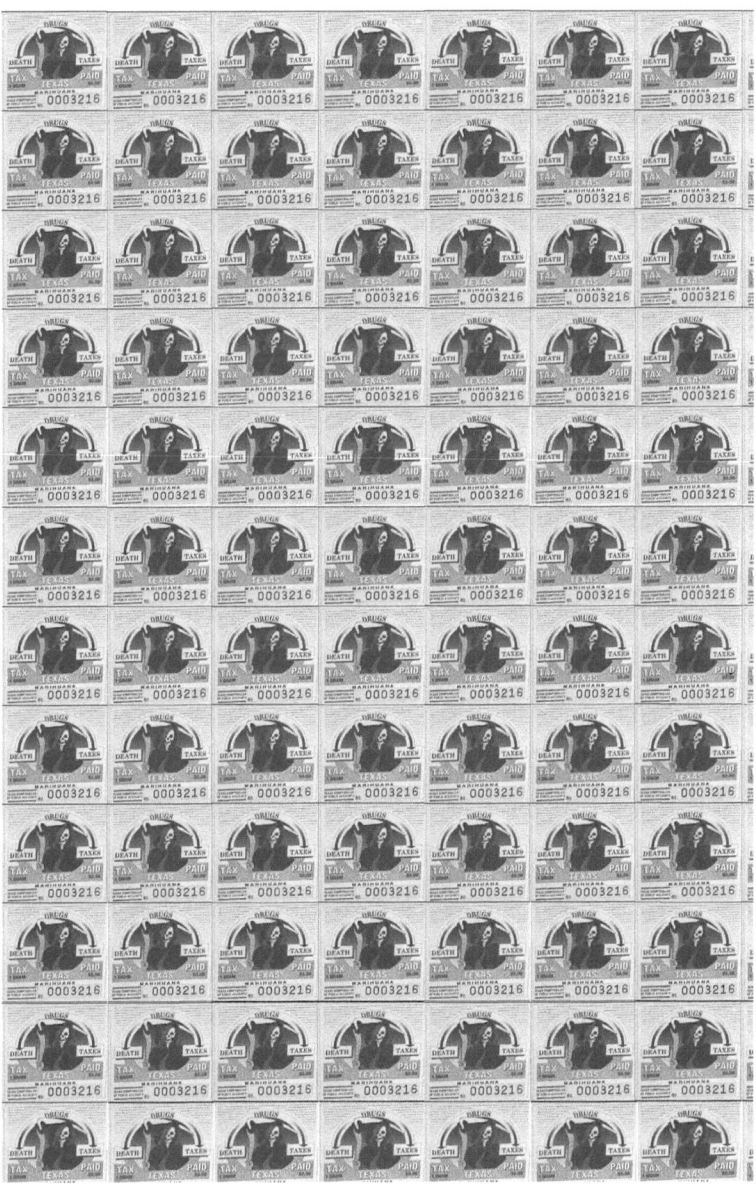

Denver Day

On Whose Watch?

I woke up Sunday morning and drove to the station about 9 o'clock where, as usual, Lieutenant MacKinney was already hours and hours and hours into his daily rigmarole.

Different shifts strung together by the ever-flowing coffee pot. Flow my coffee, Mr. Dick's policeman might have remarked, may he rest in peace. I briefed him regarding the night before, warts and all.

"People living that hellbent train of a lifestyle tend not to get hangovers. That isn't the hair of the dog, they just wake up and eat the whole bloody ox allover again," he said. "So I imagine, she won't rise and shine until noon, at best. Let's go around lunchtime to catch her at breakfast."

Knock Knock. Some commotion from within and some delay, some haggling with several locks from behind the apartment door. Chinese takeout man emerged in his underwear. "She never came home last night," he said.

"When's she due back?" the lieutenant asked.

Pizza Noir

"Well, she's working tonight at 10, and she'll probably stop by here at least to clean up before she goes in."

"Any idea where we might find her until then?" Nope, he said he didn't.

"Thanks anyway, and tell her I called if you happen to run into her." I gave him one of my cards. "And you can call me too, were it ever necessary."

We headed to the hotel where last night's end-run took place. I mentioned on the way that I met a lady sax player.

"Don't shit where you eat, Ricky," the lieutenant answered.

We pulled into the hotel parking lot, walked into the lobby, and of course the whole scene was night-and-day different from last night's brouhaha. We nodded to the front desk staffer, who was yakking away on the phone, and rode the elevator up.

Knock knock. Some delay, some shuffling about from inside, the lock clicked, and then came a woman's voice through the door, "who is it?"

"Detective Ricky Thompson with the state police, here to talk with Ms. Keri Anders."

Another moment.

Denver Day

"Coming, Ricky. Be right there, hang on."

It was her. MacKinney grimaced and muttered something about handcuffs and a body condom. She opened the door in navy sweatpants, flip-flops, and a gray tank-top. She was smoking a menthol cigarette, and the room was thick with its crispy menthol fog. She looked relatively no more worse for the miles she'd put on in the past two days or even the last 12 hours. She seemed to be the only one left in the suite.

"Some party last night," I said. "Thought we might find you here; we already tried your apartment."

"Oh yeah that's right!" she screeched. "I remember seeing you last night. And thanks for the big tip, that goes a long way."

What resilience! She wasn't even limping.

The lieutenant nodded and tipped his hat: "Miss, we need to ask you some more questions about the death of your fiance, Stephen Wang, and the two others. We want to get to the bottom of this as much as you must do. May we come in?"

It was pretty itchy in there, but the menthol cloud mitigated it somewhat, sort of I guess? She sat on the couch where she had last night been so heavily occupied herself.

"First, we want you to know, that we're not so much worried about all this drug use as a crime, per se. We know that this sort of activity is, unfortunately, irreducible from your unfortunate career choice and workplace setting," MacKinney told her. "With all that, just for now, it's only relevant insofar as its relationship as evidence with respect to the murder of the girl, and Mr. Wang, and the third, yet unidentified victim. So, again please know, it's not what we're after. This is a homicide investigation."

She considered his words, and they might have made sense to her. With strippers like her and those of similar stripes, the dynamic is often much like interviewing a child, however. Very early in my career, a county prosecutor related to me the general investigative watermark known as the "Santa Claus Rule."

That is, when interviewing juvenile witnesses for criminal investigations, the approximate benchmark for expecting credible statements from children falls along the same threshold of whether or not they still believe in Santa Claus. So as a general guideline, if they still believe in Santa Claus, they shouldn't be relied upon to give useful, dependable court testimony or witness statements. Reason being is, that such a fantastic belief indicates a child's inability to dependably make rational assessments.

When a child suffers a traumatic incident or is severely victimized, and the impact isn't psychologically stop-lossed and resolved with an experience of affirmative closure, then important parts of their development tend to stop right there at the moment of the trauma, forever or until repaired.

This seemed clearly the case with Ms. Anders, as having any sort of conversation with her made evident that something in her had stopped growing at around the age of 8. And regarding certain other realms, her psychological maturity was shunted in the early teenaged years. And everything else upstairs had stopped progressing by the time she was 20, at the oldest.

Anyway, it's hard to know if individuals like this are following your forensic logic. More broadly, it's impossible to know if coked-up strippers are lying or not, beyond the conservative approach of simply assuming that everything they say is a lie, because mindfulness of the integrity of his or her good word is not typically on the top of a junkie's list.

"It's my estimation that your fiance, and the other two, were killed when your Mr. Wang was ripped off during a drug deal. I would say it's a situation that your new friend, the man who's at your apartment right now, should take care to avoid, and a situation of which also you should be very cautious. After all, you may be our only witness. Are you able now to tell me who did it?"

Now, she might offer up a petty rival. She might claim not to remember, which would be plausible also. She might even identify additional accessories.

I looked over at the lieutenant. She considered the question for several moments. Looking back at me, she torched another menthol.

"We were in the backstage area of the Squeeze Box Club. It was last call for the bar, and the girls were still rotating through the stage. But I was done for the night and I was tipping-out to the barbacks, about to head out to an after-hours party. Stevie showed up with my dinner, and with some other stuff for some of the barbacks and other girls. That's when I heard a scream, it came from that girl."

"When I turned around she was in the floor

on top of a huge, dark-red puddle of blood. The pizza Stevie had brought for us was on the ground, and he and the other guy were both wrestling with this, like, huge Latino guy covered in tattoos."

"But the huge guy must've known karate, or something, because Stevie had jumped on his back and was strangling him and kicking him with his heavy boots, but the guy just started ramming him into the cinder-block backstage wall like some kind of wild animal, until Stevie finally let go and fell off."

"Then the guy grabbed the other girl's date by the arm and pulled him close, and, like, bear-hugged him. He made a funny sound and there was a big blood puddle where he fell. I thought that I was going to be next, at that point, so I just freaked out and ran out the back door and caught a ride to the party. I came here."

She gestured toward the couch.

"I kept waiting for Stevie to show up, but he never did. Obviously."

She said she vaguely recognized the large Latino man, having seen him around the clubs before, but that she didn't know his name, and hadn't seen him since.

Pizza Noir

We got off the elevator, again nodded to the receptionist, who was still in the throes of a gale-force phone conversation, and we walked out into the day.

"May God have mercy on her soul, Ricky," the lieutenant said. "She smells like bugspray."

He made a quick call in to the captain, then we headed directly back to Anders' apartment, to speak again with her newest cohabitant, the sublimely combative Mr. Louis Ho. Why he chose Chinese food rather than Italian-American, as his preferred coke trafficking vector, may remain a puzzle forever.

"But like I said, please understand, this is not that kind of investigation," MacKinney repeated himself to the painted lady's newest thing. "Were you at the after-party with Ms. Anders early Saturday morning?"

"Yeah. When she got there she was crying, and told us about the bad scene at the Squeeze Box. She kept watching the door and asking what time it was. She kept talking about how Stevie should be there any minute. She was upset, and I was there for her. I could sort of relate, because I knew Stevie. I used to work with him."

"Stevie's been dead less than 48 hours. The

two of you've gotten pretty heavily involved, pretty quickly," I prodded.

"She's a big girl Dick. And she has a big appetite like that way. What you saw last night is the way we do things, yeah, and Stevie would've answered your question the same way," he strutted. "That's just how we roll. Yeah yeah."

"I understand. Just thought I'd put the question. What about the person who did it? Seen him? Has anybody? Who is he?"

"A Mexican, I think his name's Alvarez, from down in the Bay Area. Not a local. His face has only popped up every once in a while, going back. I wouldn't know where to tell you to look. But yeah Keri says he ripped off Stevie and snuffed him and that girl and her date. Uh huh."

The lieutenant and I went to the diner next to the office for my lunch and his supper. By mid-afternoon, the humidity had worked itself up into a squall in-between dinner rushes. I ordered a BLT with brown mustard and iced tea. The lieutenant got the pesto spaghetti with a coffee chaser. Through the diner's glass windows, we watched some guy walk by who looked like he'd had nothing but gasoline to drink that day.

"Ricky, you know I can smell through walls," MacKinney said, turning back to face me. "I don't know if I believe the large-and-conveniently-murderous-out-of-towner-Mexican story or the tooth fairy either," he grumbled, stirring the basil-based sauce with his fork. "So good luck. Let me know what you find out."

Objects in Motion

A huge glossy fair-skinned brunette with a prominent, glistening, blood-red, heart-shaped tattoo on her stage-right cleavage; on top of a fresh coat of glossy black paint; on top of many previous paint layers, adorned the cinderblock

Denver Day

exterior of MC's Ale House.

Sources told me it was a good place to look for Martin Alvarez, because of the intracoastally transient nature of its many two-wheeled regulars. Even on a Sunday afternoon.

He wasn't hiding. Sitting casually, at the bar, he still looked physically bowed-up. His body mass dwarfed his bar stool and the double rocks glass he held. He was watching the sports news on one of the rafter-mounted T.V.s. It was pretty early yet and still pleasantly empty here, cool and roomy. Barkeep asked if I'd wanted anything, so I ordered a stout ale before I introduced myself.

"You probably don't want to hear this, but a local stripper and her coked-up Chinese gay blade boyfriend say you killed three people early yesterday morning."

I handed him my card. He looked at it, took a few notes, and gave it back.

"Well, as you're probably guessing, it wasn't me. You want to talk to my lawyer?" he answered.

"Won't be necessary today. But it's my job to haul somebody in, ultimately. So far the best candidate I have is the happy couple. Why do you think they would see fit to hang this business on the likes of you?" I asked.

Pizza Noir

It was obvious that he was physically and mentally capable of doing what they accused him of doing. But it was also clear that he was probably way too reasonable and intelligent to grease three zites at a titty bar, then wait around town to get roped for it. He drained his glass. The barkeep picked it up, adding ice.

"I'd say you've got a stripper and her boyfriend, ripping off her other boyfriend. Blow and a jilted lover, in her office, at closing time, no more no less," he answered.

"And why paint me a daisy? I have a theory: I like to fuck hookers, and I used to fuck her all the time before she got used up. And her morons never liked it."

A fair assessment from Martin Alvarez. The barman set a new pour in front of him.

"Thank you then, Mr. Alvarez. I appreciate your time."

Some of it is produced locally, and some stuff comes through regional domestic transportation rights-of-way, but much of the gear, the good stuff, and the like, with which essentially all of my suspects and their associates fully gird themselves in to fuck-off and die, comes up the California coast into the Northwest from Mexico, although the Great White North is an increasingly competitive black market source, particularly for heroin, prescription drugs, and other blues.

Because of the criminal qualification of such imports, it has always been a hot black market out here, as the domestic market for these products is extremely and increasingly lucrative for their import.

The only way to beat it is to quell the source, which requires total system organization and divine intervention, and so is the subject of a separate dissertation about crime interdiction and citizen education.

Anyway, our database paints the various logistics in our neck of the woods, with respect to what groups are involved, and by approximate annual weight of traffic, for example. The domestic motorcycle clubs have historical precedent herewith, but as the cartels from south of the border have grown to leviathan levels of power, scope, and influence in the decades before and after the turn of the 21st century, the foreign logistical operations are increasingly competitive among the legacy domestic routes and traffic.

Political decisions therewith are policed and regulated internally by the respective black market syndicates. Various states, because of their own arm's-length laws, are often institutionally disenfranchised from the intervention of said black markets. Steadily as always, both production and demand continue their incline, and not just on the West Coast.

Still, it seemed like Alvarez was probably not my guy, regardless of what he did for a day job. Moreover, it seemed to me that this case was thoroughly downstream of any and all political interactivity among major narcotics syndicates. Furthermore, and most importantly here, where the pizza man's coke came from was probably irrelevant anyway, as far as the prosecutors would care.

From MC's, I drove to the office of the county coroner Dixie Thompson, who also happens to be my ex wife. She said nobody yet had claimed the cadaver in the suit. He had no identification nor paperwork except for a small wad amounting to $900 in fifty- and hundred-dollar bills, a full pack of cigarettes, and half a dozen eight balls. He wore a very nice European suit with a tailor's signature stitched in Cyrillic

Denver Day

lettering with gold thread: "В. Конычу."

"The girl's family's been ringing the phone off the hook. As for Mr. Wang, his people just said call 'em when we're ready to let him go. Of course, the suit doesn't have a date for the prom yet," she said. "But they're all three packed up and ready to ship, whenever you give us the word. You want to have another look, Rick?"

"Yep. Roll 'em out for me." She handed me a yardwork-slash-bird flu mask, and pulled the covers off the three bodies which were parked together, side by side, back in the back.

The girl had changed out of her dancing gear and into cling-fit denim pants and a white belly shirt which read "naughty for nice" in big screen-printed pink letters. She had the requisite tattoos, butterflies on both ankles, an ivy tramp stamp on her lower back, a bangle on the right wrist, and a small bar code on the nape of her neck.

She had long fingernails, with an hybrid mud of cocaine and blood underneath the ones on her pinkies. Stevie Wang's whiffer nails were also manicured to deliver similar payloads, but he had no tattoos. Dixie had put Wang's Land's End windbreaker back on him after the autopsy, but his and the girl's jewelry remained in metal bowls on a nearby table.

The man in the suit was not dancing. All dressed up with nowhere to go. He was probably in his early thirties or so, with a shaved head. Unlike Wang, who was pretty skinny, this guy was fit and beefy, protein shakes for certain and probably anabolic steroids as well. He was without tattoos, but his ballsack and dickhead had large gauged piercings, Dixie dutifully reported.

"And all three of them were pretty well totally shaved," she said. "Saved me a little time in the post-mortem."

"Dixie, that's your department. I'll focus on the live ones," I said. "Is there anything else besides this guy's tackle that you feel is worth mentioning?"

"No. There's a big palm-sized birthmark on the side of his torso," she said. "Not uncommon among Eastern Block honkies. Coffee?" she asked.

"Sure."

I thought I had the case all squared away for my Monday-morning briefing with the lieutenant. He let me talk for a while before he burst my bubble.

"I presume Stevie Wang's and Louis Ho's cocaine salads amount to small-quantity end-user sales from a much longer ride up the coast, the history of which is another investigation for another guy on some other day," I said. "Up through the Bay Area on two chrome wheels. More to the point here, though, I'd say Ho took Wang's position as Anders' blow supplier and manager of her end-user "homestead" action. And I'd say, that during the changing of the guard, Wang met his maker. I'd pin the actual act on Ho, or some goon even stupider than he is, with Anders as an accessory and probably the instigator. In light of the strong supporting circumstantial evidence, and because she admitted to being at the crime scene when it happened, we can go ahead and draw up some charges on Anders," I said. "If it wasn't her, she probably knows who it was, and she'll tell us when we put the squeeze on her."

But MacKinney had a look about him, and for good reasons, as it turned out.

"Uh, Rick, there's something else. And big, so hold on to your hat," the lieutenant said. "Yes, we can talk about bringing them in, you're right, but you need to look at this weirdness first. It's new information and it drastically changes things."

He handed me a stack of reports from the printer on his desk. Multiple agencies. Murder investigations. All strippers. From as far south as San Diego and one so close as King County.

"San Diego to Seattle, and points in between, Rick, and look at the date on them all. I was telephoning colleagues up and down Highway 101, saying hey, we got a dead stripper, maybe due to a local market turf issue, you know, asking them if they're noticing any major narco-traffic sea change at hand that may correlate. Just typical background oversight. But on the first call I made, Sacramento asks me when we black-bagged our three. Turns out they had the same thing on the same night, early Saturday morning, and so forth."

"Ricky, I was looking for some related trend in the black market. Not on the goddamned cud circuit," he vented heat. "This is bloody not good."

Dead strippers in a dozen-odd cities on the same night. Strangled, shot, bludgeoned, or several like ours with their throats cut. And he was right, this was a hairpin turn in the investigation. From isolated street-level violence among the unwashed, to an organized, full-blown, psychopathic interstate blood bath.

You can't really categorize it as a serial killing if the crimes all happened at the same time at widely separated locations. Not yet; it would have to happen again to qualify. For now, it's more of a wave event than a series. But it does become multi-jurisdictional, and the gang and narcotics details will want to whip out their very own bigs and shinies.

Since it is now an interstate case, the posties will sprinkle donuts allover the place. And when the 6 o'clock news crews dip their taint into it, there might not be enough popcorn.

Denver Day

Uh Oh

"Brown strippers, black strippers, yellow strippers, red strippers," MacKinney said, with his usual awareness of political correctness. "If it were narcotics related, we could establish moxy. I'm starting to wish it were, but I don't think it is. You got legacy MC circuit girls, Latinas, street-level dope dealers, freelance dancers. It's a hodgepodge, Rick. And this is happening irrespective of whose dope it is or whom gets it from who."

So I telephoned the sax player. Tina. Tina Tina. "Heya Tina. It's Rick Thompson here. Coffee?" I asked her.

"Lunch," she countered.

It was about that time anyway. She met me at the diner next to my office, and we dined. She was a hand shorter than me, with thick, neck-length, almost-black, straight hair. She ordered a mid-rare steak and a coke. So me too. This pleased me, as I hadn't had a steak in a long time.

"You solve the murder yet?" she asked me.

"Well. No. Thought I was about to, but a twist in the plot and it turns out to be a little more complicated," I answered.

"How so?" she queried.

"About two dozen other murdered strippers, all in the same small hours early Saturday, all up and down the West Coast," I told her.

"Nooooooo shit," she said. She looked down at her steak. "Well. That's what I call organized crime," she looked back up from her plate and smiled. "It wasn't me!"

Tina said she recognized all three of our victims from the nightly anon at the after-hours lounge but that she couldn't recall any notable personal run-ins with them.

"We're listening to every rumor, any random observation at all from anybody on this case because it's different. It's not linear, it was more like a burst, and at this point we're guessing," I continued. "Some people are starting to suspect no less than science fiction."

"I'll ask the band if they've seen anything, and if I see you again, I'll let you know what they had to say," she smiled.

"Great," I answered, moving the subject away from the topic of my work. "How long have you been playing that horn?"

"About 25 years. But I've been doing it for a

living for only about five. I used to work for the Forest Service, but I got fired after some tax collector found roaches in the ashtray of one of our trucks. It had to be either me or the whole unit to walk the plank for it. So as the squad leader I took the black ball," she explained. "I miss the outdoors, but this is better than selling insurance."

She grabbed her purse and excused herself to the restroom. I payed the check while she was in there. She told me to telephone anytime, whenever I got my next break from work. I walked her out to her car, then drove back to the office to see how the lieutenant was getting along with his lunch date. Anders was in character, sitting around wearing sweatpants, flip-flops and a tank top, and smoking menthols. Louis Ho, yeah, yo, he was sitting there looking nervous.

"She had thought she was pregnant, but her period came Friday, so she was celebrating that night. She had a good night for tips, and met that other guy at the club that night too, the stocky bald guy," Anders said. "We were all rolling over to the hotel for an after-hours drink."

"Who was the possible father?" I asked Anders. She said she didn't know, and that maybe the girl herself hadn't known. "I mean, she was a working girl, and she worked hard, so it can get kind of complicated with stuff like that. I mean, she even dated a lot of the same people I do."

Oh, brother, aye. Ho said he was pretty sure he wasn't the father, uh-huh. MacKinney pulled me into his office.

"They were undoubtedly spooked at the sight of three bodies. They had to explain it somehow, just like we're trying to. I believe they arrived at their story about Alvarez because it was plausible, and they didn't want to get roped into what appeared to be a drug deal gone south. Alvarez's associations are not direct connections to Stevie Wang's or Louis Ho's coke sources, so hanging it on him makes a good red herring, even by tweaker logic," he said. "I think that's the long and the short of why they named him, and there is some old jealousy still there, perhaps, and Alvarez might have been at the Box that night. One minute it was business as usual, and then someone happens to walk back there and find three fresh ones in the floor."

"I don't know who or what she saw, but I don't think she saw Alvarez do it, like she said she did, because I don't think he did it. Especially not in light of these new, more widespread developments," I said.

"Well, and, the general storyline everywhere else is similar. This seems to have gone down right under broad nightlight, and for all 21 homicides at umpteen locations the total number of surviving witnesses is one. Anyway, what'd you have for lunch?"

"Bloody steak," I answered. "Tina said she'd ask the band if they had any observations about our victims or witnesses or characters of interest otherwise."

"She seen anything?" he asked.

"She'd seen the Russian suit and the Asian pizza man before, but never had any conversations with either of them. She recognized the girl's face too, regular working-girl-slash-dancer, like Anders," I said. "But no smoking gun, eh. Anything from the other agencies?"

"Not as such. Much like our own, just dead strippers coated with coke and jazz. All the victim's purses had tampons in them, and all good bears shit in the woods," he said. "I'm calling Rich Hays at the Seattle Bureau, he used to work for the state police up there for a lot of years. He can put some good English on it when he notifies his people, hopefully we can all move along as seamlessly as possible."

He picked up the phone and punched up 10 digits. "Howdy Rich, Danny MacKinney . . . . not bad . . . oh, yeah. Yes, she's fat and happy . . . yep . . . yep. No, this is business. Hey it looks like we have a thing down here."

I rang up our old lady the coroner.

"Dixie, I need you to make some phone calls to some of your colleagues." I gave her the various jurisdictions involved in the case.

"Turns out about 21 people were killed, about the same time as our three, all along the I-5. The only two of the whole lot who weren't strippers were our Russian suit and the pizza man. Do please feel free to scrupulously network this new development as you see fit among your circles. Anything new otherwise?"

"Nope. Just that daddy wants his little girl back to plant her. He called again this afternoon. The other guy still has no takers. I'll catch up with you after I ponder the day's new set of facts," she said.

I went ahead working the phones in earnest. Vancouver's freeze-block-slash-cricket-bat ordeal was the biggest quazi-Indocanadian sports-themed mess I've ever been privy to, with two girls aged 20 and 21 on the business end of it.

Age and gender demographics of the victims were about the same at every crime scene, typically 18-to-32-year-old female nightclub dancers, young and bloody, either in the parking lots or dressing rooms, at their shifts' ends (our case was the only place involving any male victims).

Anyway, Vancouver detectives there did recover the freeze block duct taped to a cricket bat (a spanking paddle that had been intentionally drill-perforated in some former and less macabre of its incarnations). But it was not good for fingerprints, and what might have been the victim's footprints were quite indistinguishable from what might have been the perpetrator's, or those of the monkey next door; it had been raining like an MF up there all week. It might as well have happened three decades ago as far as the Vancouver weather was concerned. And in a strip club parking lot full of high people of questionable means, there were no witnesses either.

Longview looked like a .357 hollow point or

better. The victim was the last person out of the building, a stripper and key-holding employee, and she got it in the dressing room. Nobody found her until they came to open up around noon the next day. No apparent witnesses. A similar caliber was used in Salem, the statements indicated the girls were filtering out, wrapping up their shifts, and suddenly one of them comes around the corner to see another of them shot dead. But it was loud as hell in there and nobody even could recall hearing any shots fired.

Seattle involved a single 12-gauge shotgun blast to the face at close range, which totally disintegrated the head of its target. There was some lead field load and one anonymous, spent, high velocity shell found at the scene in the parking lot. Like most of the other locations, there were no eyewitnesses forthcoming, just people surprised by a body. A pattern was clearly emerging that the perpetrators of these homicides were effectively using crowds, and darkness, and general latenight drug-addled shift-change entropy as cover for their quick work.

Portland was a shotgun also, to the chest at close range, and also in the parking lot, blowing a six-inch hole in the victim. None of her peers saw that happen either. A high velocity field load of some sort; this was probably a 20 gauge, although there was no spent shell found at that scene.

Beaverton, like our mess, involved an edged instrument, a box-cutter razor, which was left in the victim, who was found in her vehicle the next morning when the club's clean-up and day crew arrived.

In Eugene, the victim was run-through with a cheap, plastic-handled machete, which was also left lodged in the body, that was found in a locked restroom stall, was accidentally discovered by one of the club's patrons. And nobody saw shit there either, but there was an anonymous swish of blood on the floor where someone had rolled out from under the wall of the locked toilet stall.

Medford's perpetrator was a Third-Reich-like .22-caliber round right into the ear; a small pistol of relatively little noise; the victim was slumped over a coke mirror, at a booth in a loud and crowded strip club, with several other people sitting with her at the same booth doing the same stuff off of the same surface. But nobody could name seeing anything there either. One minute she's right there, and the next she's slumped over dead. At first they thought it was an overdose, and had supposed the blood from the bullet wound was coming from her nose, not her ear. Anyway, someone hopped over the wall of an abutting booth, or someone crawled under the tables, the local investigators figured.

In these crowded dark spots, all these killers had to do was blink or turn their bodies slightly to cover themselves with the cloak and cover of night and thickly anonymous crowds.

Going south, California's cases were quite the same as those in the great northwest. In Santa Cruz, a .22 into the ear also, and, surprisingly, the bartender saw the whole thing, yet to no avail. Some dude in an overcoat walks in, orders a beer, drinks it, gets up, walked over to a stripper sitting at the bar, puts one in her ear, and is out the door before the guy can even get his ass hopped over the bar. He didn't even have a good guess at the height or race of the assailant. Nothing.

And in Sunnyvale, a .22 in the ear of a girl sitting in a dressing room stall, in the back of the house. Dod kalm, nobody saw or heard anything.

In both Oxnard and San Jose, a dancer was

Denver Day

picked off the stripper stage with perfectly sniped head shots, with net zero suspects. Found in the floor of the club in San Jose was the brass from a spent .44-caliber shell.

San Francisco was a buck knife in the room of an hotel next door to the victim's nightclub. The room had been booked in her name using her credit card. The front desk reported only seeing her when she checked in.

In Los Gatos, an all nude dancer found her friend in the parking lot, having followed to investigate after her buddy had gone to the parking lot to fetch her cigarettes from her car, but didn't return. Blunt-force trauma with a metal baseball bat.

Santa Ana was a sawed-off 12-gauge shotgun, which was left right there at the scene, still loaded, in the short-order kitchen of an all-nude bar. When he nearly tripped over it, the cook back there was as surprised at the body as the rest of the staff.

In Long Beach a girl fell dead on stage, and the autopsy showed recent ingestion of a significant amount of rat poison with her last meal of fast food.

Los Angeles was a pre-after-hours-party

speed-ball overdose in the dressing room.

And in San Diego, two topless girls just disappeared at some point in the night. And they're still gone.

So ours was the only one that involved men down; Santa Cruz was the only place where anybody actually claimed to have seen it happen (if not counting ours), and San Diego was the only place with no body in hand. San Deigo was also the only agency that claimed to have a solid lead, the lieutenant said. So I called them first.

Denver Day

Catch as Catch Can

Detective Joseph Lopez, of the San Diego city force: "Our chief tells me this is part of a greater incident. Now, as a point of information, you know very well that strippers do, in fact, just disappear from time to time. In San Diego it's not like the ongoing shit storm down the road in T.J., but it happens. Anyway, here's what I got: Two weeks ago we had a confrontation between a womens roller derby squad and some of the people working at a club down here. One of the derby girls ended up in a box. You're familiar with roller derby."

"Anyway, more or less, the scene at the bar seemed to be business as usual to us at first, but I have started researching that derby geography further because of the possible connection to Saturday morning's killings. The girl killed two weeks ago was a member of the Bloody Rollers outfit out of Phoenix, and there was a derby-circuit gathering down here that weekend, and among many other squads the Bloody Rollers were in from out of town."

"The Bloody Rollers comprise a decent collective felony rap. Still, many on their roster are lady knights lily-white. Anyway, they're all pretty tough gals and there's a lot of allegiance and rivalries and trysts and general drama to be expected among the teams and throughout the circuit at large. The night that girl was killed down here, she and/or members of her party had gotten crossways with some or another group of strippers and their people, and the shark soup boiled over fast."

"But, for me to say this set off some mass revenge killing of 21 unrelated victims all the way from here to Washington State is asking too much of the imagination. So, rather than revenge on that measure, it's more likely that some yet-unnamed group might have just used it as an excuse to go totally nanners."

"Thanks Lopez. I appreciate your input on this, moving forward," I said. "My lieutenant is contacting the Bureau in Seattle, what so the posties don't shit rolling donuts on us for failure to notify them about an interstate development. So I give you fair warning now, that they'll be in touch with you office in the morning. Because nobody else has squat, aside from what you guys have down there. In the meantime, I'd love to see the file on the skater girl homicide."

Denver Day

"All right. I'll fax you some stuff. I've started digging around on the Bloody Rollers and the derby circuit in general, and I've got a call in to Maricopa County about their hometown girls. I'll give a teleconference debriefing for all agencies involved so far, if it's necessary," he said. "Spread the word on that for me, as you may. And if you don't hear from me by tomorrow afternoon, call me back. What about the media?"

"The beans are still in the pot for now. I guess the cases are geographically far enough apart for local media outlets not to have noticed the pattern yet. Sooner or later they might, though. As for the posties, it would be the general exception to their general guidelines for them to contact the media directly, if it's in their best interest," I said. "Anyway, just be prepared. I phoned you first, since you've got the only lead. I mean, we only found out yesterday that this whole deal was bad as well as nationwide."

Next, I called Santa Cruz, where the investigator said he'd interviewed the barkeep the day before, and surprise, surprise, surprise, it had happened in a dark bar, loud bar, crowded bar, smokey bar full of dark, loud, crowded, smokey bar people. Their witness couldn't confirm gender, race, age, size, weight, height, nor wind or rain. The person working the door also didn't know jack-diddley.

Someone blended in and moved quickly, mixed with a little element of surprise and a lot of background noise. Snake eyes at the only location with a witness.

MCSO and Phoenix P.D. got back to Lopez, to report that the skater girl who was killed in San Diego, Jessica Roller, had no criminal history at all, not out of Arizona or California or anywhere else.

She'd shared an address with two of her teammates, Becca Roller, also 31 (formerly Becca Reaugh), and Veronica Roller, 42, formerly Veronica Martinez and also formerly a Navajo Nation highway patrol officer.

Becca Reaugh had spent three years with the Arizona Department of Corrections, following a DV incident on her 22nd birthday that resulted in her shooting and killing her boyfriend in their apartment in Scottsdale. As for the present day, both Becca and Veronica were accounted for in Phoenix, and going about Jessica's final arrangements.

Both Veronica and Becca were present when Jessica died, and both gave witness statements to police that were vague and short. Becca attested that she was in the restroom when it went down, and Veronica said she was beating on some guy with a pool cue for calling Jessica a hooker, when her friend received her death blows, she said she turned around from her busy work to see Jessica's head caved into the floor.

It's not unusual to have this sort of general forensic disarray when there's a barroom brawl gone too far south. The facsimile from Lopez in San Diego included several other witness statements; from some of the girls' friends and teammates, the bar staff and other onlookers who were at hand. They'd made no arrests nor officially named any suspects. It was just a brawl at a sharp-edged roadhouse out on the highway, and one of those lady skaters got her skull squashed, that's all. Nobody saw anything specific before or after the dust cleared, R.I.P. Jessica Roller, age 31, formerly Jessica Hollander, of Phoenix.

Several of her teammates, several skaters from other teams, and several of the girls and boys working at the place were bloody, black, and blue, and their statements were all pretty muddy too. Lopez also sent me a Bloody Rollers roster;

he noted that any list of staff at the roadhouse didn't really exist because the staff were all freelancers.

The barkeep, dancers, and waitstaff were all compensated strictly on a tips-oriented, on-the-fly, cash-only, third party basis. The general consensus was of a quickly escalating dust-up, followed by general confusion among a crowd, followed by the fast flight of everybody involved excepting Jessica, her answerable teammates, and the overwhelmed bar staff.

Illustrating further forensic entropy and additionally diluting our only investigative break to date, the two dancers who went missing out of the San Diego club on October 11 disappeared from a different bar in a different part of town.

I disseminated a memorandum to the other agencies involved, advising of the teleconference set for the following day. Lopez spent much of his Monday evening researching the travel logistics among the derby circuit and its juxtaposition among the geography of the 11 October killings.

If those killings were some sort of retribution for the Roller homicide, it was nevertheless a rather obtuse response, to target a group of people who shared nothing more than a certain loose demographic affiliation with whoever might have killed Ms. Roller the week before, nevermind the disparate geography .

I briefed MacKinney regarding my convo with Detective Lopez: "He sent me a case file summary for the Jessica Roller homicide. Nobody saw anything. He's communicating with the Bloody Rollers squad's hometown handlers in Maricopa County. Also, the two girls missing out of San Diego disappeared from a different bar, and as far as anyone knows they weren't at the roadhouse when the Jessica Roller was killed, or ever. Lopez scheduled a teleconference for tomorrow for all agencies involved from Arizona and along the West Coast," I said. "What did your Seattle federal buddies say?"

"Told us to keep them abreast of how things go, and of any breaks in the case. I let them know about the San Diego lead, so they can check into that deal," the lieutenant said. "Would you mind getting another barometer reading out of the local jungle tonight?"

About 6 o'clock, the coroner's office phoned. The consensus, Dixie said, included just some general circumstantial stuff in addition to the common locations and demographics that were already apparent. Mainly, that all of the death blows, whether by gunshot or blunt force or blade or poison were all quite professionally done, or at least effective, as far as can deals like that go. Beyond that, there was nothing much new, she said.

"It would seem that there are, at this very moment, a great many extremely effective perpetrators on the loose. How about you might watch out for a repeat there, Ricky," she said.

It was dusky and drizzling when I left the office. Such a possibility of a second act was dark, because of the apparent ease and stealth associated with the darkness of Saturday morning's affair. For now a repeat seemed the best chance for any investigative break, though, and that's admittedly pretty dark thinking too, I thought to myself.

When I walked into the diner next door for a bite, Joe was in there cheating on himself, drinking the diner's slightly thicker and slightly hotter coffee, compared to that of his kiosk pot.

I joined him at the bar and ordered scrambled eggs and iced tea and we shot the shit about work and weather. There was more rain in

Denver Day

the forecast. The waitress brought my eggs and tea, and refilled Joe's cup. She smiled at us. I watched her turn and hang an order ticket with a click on a stainless steel wheel in the expediter's window.

Outside an ambulance siren came and went. The front page of the newspaper was filled with election clutter, and the sports page discussed the nearing and unavoidable end of baseball season. Joe worked the crossword.

After about an hour's down time, I headed for MC's Ale House. It was about half past eight. The fleshy and glossy brunette on the front of the building winked at me through the ambient moisture under the glowing neons and black lights. The parking lot contained mostly chrome two-wheelers as usual. I nodded at Alvarez, who was holding court at the end of the bar. The pool tables were all occupied. The house music was potted up much louder than I had experienced during my daytime visit.

The place wasn't jam packed, but it was bustling. The waitresses all wore uniforms similar to the one painted on the girl who was painted on the front of the building; mascara moles, polka-dotted bows, black fishnets, and plaited skirts.

Pizza Noir

I sat down and ordered an ale. The girls here were working as waitresses, not dancers. This wasn't even so much as a topless club, the girls didn't reek of doom or foreboding, and they all seemed to be there of their own accord. The air of the club was breathable, nearly crisp.

The waitresses were clear eyed, and the patrons were more interested in their conversations and pool games instead of just constantly snorkeling up train dust. The barkeep drew me a chocolate oatmeal stout. I asked him if he'd noticed anything unusual since Saturday morning's incident over at the Squeeze Box Club.

No, but anybody of or related to the local stripping racket had to be concerned, he opined. I informed him that there were other strippers / dancers killed on the same night in cities all along the West Coast all the way down to San Diego.

I watched the sports news playing on the big screen hanging behind the bar for a while. I stood up, left cash on the bar and headed for the door, angling next to the Squeeze Box. Alvarez nodded again as I made my way out.

It was flat-out raining hard when I got back outside. At about 9:45, I pulled into the parking lot of the Squeeze Box. Unlike MC's, it was not bustling. The bartender was working by herself, with only one bar back on hand, who was stacking bottle boxes in the back of the house. There were no patrons near the stage, and no one on the stage, and the house music was hushed.

A small group huddled around drinks at the end of the bar, also occasionally gandering up at the sports news on the hanging T.V. She explained that, on Monday nights, the club was basically just a dimly lit swinging door tavern with not enough crowd or demand that can be expected on the Box's busier nights of the week. Time was, she said, they weren't open on Mondays whatsoever.

I asked if she'd heard anything interesting about Saturday morning's killings: "Well, I am one of the managers, and it has been business as usual for the past three days, detective," she said. "But Keri Anders phoned me today, tells me you're investigating some other ones."

I gave her my card. I watched her eyes when she talked, and studied her face. She was sharp, wary, wry, attractive though slightly weathered, but not in a bad way, and generally wise with respect to her station.

"Do you have any contacts with or have you heard from, any of the other incident locations along the coast?" I trawled.

"Well, it's been three days. Word does travel through the grapevine. But I don't get out much, and I don't have any sister-wives in any of those cities, or here in Tacoma either as far as that goes," she said.

"What do you think about Anders?" I asked her.

"Well you know, she's not up on that stage splitting atoms. She's an addict and a whore and probably not long for this world," she said. "But I really don't think she's made of the stuff required to chop people up. She's probably too mentally adrift to execute anything like that. But, it is true that she doesn't know any better than to hang out with losers."

"OK. I hear you. Keep your eye on the doors around here. Nobody's made any arrests yet," I said, standing. I tipped my hat and looked toward the group at the far end of the bar, not recognizing any of them. The rain had let up somewhat, albeit temporarily, as I walked to the car. There were just a few vehicles, and nobody but me in the parking lot.

I pulled out of the lot and headed toward my next stop, drove past the airlock motel on my

Denver Day

way to the Diddler On The Roof, which was not slumbering like the Squeeze Box. It was a different doorman than my last visit here, I think, but the guy had a similar style and asked a similar cover charge.

This club was working dancers on a Monday although it was not the jam-packed coke den I'd encountered Saturday night, and the acts weren't rotating through the stripper pier as rapidly. It was more of an after-work business crowd than a full-barreled Saturday-night shit show.

Anyway, I enjoyed another pint and watched one of the girl's acts, a redhead wearing baby blue. I didn't recognize her. I struck up a conversation with the bartender, noting that it seemed like a decent crowd for a Monday.

"The show must go on, detective. You guys arrest anybody yet?" he answered.

"Nope. You hearing any scuttle-butt?" I asked.

"Only that it didn't just happen in Tacoma," he said. "We've got our heavy-lifting staff working extra hours, more closely watching the girls, and keeping an eye on the doors you know."

From there, I went across the street to the

motel for some jazz. It was about 11 by then.

I ordered a soda and whatever the lady with the sax wanted. I waved to the band who were riding out a harried fusion piece. The horns were good, and they circulated a warm wind throughout the room at about hip level. She came over when the number ended, holding the drink that I'd sent her.

"You think they could do without you for the rest of the night?" I smiled.

"They might," she smiled back. "You hungry?"

We worked on our drinks. This hotel lounge also didn't contain the mayhem that it had during my previous visit, but it wasn't that time of night yet. We drank up, she packed up her horn, and we went to a nearby drive-through burger place. A slightly-rained-on girl hung our slightly-rained-on beanburgers and sodas from my driver-side window.

We sat there and listened to the drizzle and traffic, eating our midnighters. She said the band had nothing to report. I told her about the lead out of San Diego and suggested she might ask her band mates if they'd seen any derby girls hanging about looking fishy. "Will do," she said.

Denver Day

    We finished our late dinner, I drove her to her apartment, and she asked me up for a nightcap. We listened to the rain and the radio while we shared a bottle of pinot grigio. We screwed on her couch and fell asleep sharing the wet spot.

Ancient History

I got to the office about 7:30 on Tuesday morning. The lieutenant had been there since about five. I called down to San Diego, and Lopez said he was pretty much ready for the 10 o'clock phoner. I sent out another inter-agency memo confirming it.

"You're early Rick," MacKinney said. I went into my office to prep some meeting notes. At ten, the lieutenant and myself, and detectives from Vancouver, Portland, Salem, Seattle PD, the Seattle feds, Beaverton, Eugene, Medford, Los Gatos, Santa Ana, Long Beach, L.A., Oxnard, San Jose, Santa Cruz, Sunnyvale, San Francisco, and Longview, all got on the horn. Among others.

Hays from the bureau opened up and said hello with some data he'd queried up overnight, on female homicide stats among the West Coast's nightlife for the past five years. It didn't help.

San Diego still had the only jump but that was quickly cooling off.

"Basically, keep your eyes peeled for derby girls with crazy eyes," Lopez said. "I might give the same advice to nearly anybody anywhere, but unless somebody has new info, it's all we have.

Denver Day

We're doing as much as we can to find the girls, since we're the only place without coroner's evidence. I'll keep everyone posted on that. And Mr. Hays, if you guys at the bureau have anything to offer toward that end, please bring it on down."

Lopez continued, debriefing the party line about the Jessica Roller case. His, ours and several other agencies, had all come up with various lists of derby teams and their rosters among other potentially related connection networks, and had been keeping various data servers warm for the past day in searching and correlating criminal histories. With that, the meeting started to sound like an apocalyptic sports desk.

"For whatever reason, ours was the only place with any male victims. An unidentified thug in a Russian tailor-made suit, and a local pizza-slash-cocaine deliveryman," I put in my two cents. "So if anyone finds organized Russian fingerprints along the trail, please make a note of it. And also Asian food deliverers; as we have encountered more than one on this case."

After the teleconference, I phoned in a message to the Navajo Nation police, then continued my general digging. Logistically, if the girls had wanted to mobilize some sort of full-coastal killing tirade, it would have been fairly easy, in terms of networked boots on the ground, because the teams are pretty much everywhere these days, with a huge underground following.

The nearest to here were our own local lovelies, the Davey Jones Lickers. I heard tell that they regularly practiced in a warehouse area off I-5 down in south Tacoma, and I determined that there was no time like the present to get down there and see if anyone had any suspicious tattoos.

For lunch I had fueled up my canister with coffee from the office pot and set out to watch the Lickers at practice. The rain continued with the onset of winter, and the coffee fought a losing battle with the soppy chill. I was surprised at how many people were gathered in the bleachers just for a team practice. The practice scene and the girls' groupies concocted quite a hell of a circus. The air was electric in the warehouse with vibration from slick hard rubber wheels on the bank-boards.

I could see the why of the crowd; watching a practice was probably nearly as hot as watching an actual contest. Those women were like stout, corporeal versions of the lady painted on the front wall of MC's. They were obviously tough, and right capable of being as mean as they needed to be. I sat down about three quarters of the way up the bleachers, and sipped from my cylinder of coffee. The dudes next to me were making betting books. I handed them a Franklin and asked them for an odds sheet, which they obliged.

The ladies broke up their session at about 2 o'clock, and I walked down to get a convo with the squad captain. She was as tall as me with her skates on and was probably a barefoot five-feet-eight-inches. She had hockey legs and nice overall muscle mass, and she was good looking, sweaty and red-headed as she was. I greeted her as she sat and started undoing her skates.

"Detective Rick Thompson of the state police homicide unit. You're looking sharp out there," I said.

"Thank you," she panted. "Who are you looking for?"

I told her there was a deadly bar fight down in San Diego about 10 days ago which had involved some of her circuit peers, and that I was running down leads on it.

"Did you all go down to San Diego for that

confab?" I asked.

"I didn't but some of our girls might have. I did hear about that girl getting her head smushed, that it was a jilted lover thing, a HEAVY HEAVY HEAVY lesbian-lover-crime-of-passion-and-jealousy act, out of nowhere, at some bar. Who knows if that's true. In life, Ricky, things boil over like that sometimes. And there's just nothing anybody can do about it," she said.

She pawed my coat. "It's nice to meet you detective. My name's Sandy."

It was nice to meet Sandy, too. And she was of course right. Back in my newspaper days, for example, I'd covered an incident involving a motorcycle collision; it was a major annual poker run up in Nevada, and two riders from two clubs meeting at some point on some old mountain highway both saw the same shade of crimson at the same time, and they dialed each other over and out, head-on. They had recognized death's most becoming gesture in each others' eyes and click just like that, they delivered themselves by way of the straightest line between point A and point B. Either that, or it was a freak accident.

And what was the reason, here on earth in the flesh? Love? Revenge? It doesn't really matter after the fact. Sandy was right, sometimes people just get reaped and shit is to be expected to happen at any time, as a general rule. Stuff goes down that's just plain bloody and spooky for no good reason with no straight explanation and it occurs often enough that one is wise to get used to it. I think the proper jingoism is to "get smart."

"I know what you mean," I answered. "You wanna go somewhere and chat about it?"

"OK, let me grab my gym bag," she said. "I'll drive."

I walked with her to the locker room, then we headed out to the parking lot, where she keyed the door to an orange bug, and waved me into the passenger seat. It was a diesel, and while we waited for compression she opened me a cold can of beer from a cooler in the back seat, and she pried one open for herself. Then Sandy Licker put that bug in gear, switched on the headlights, and pulled out of the parking lot.

"Basically, Jessica Roller was the wife of her roommate and teammate, Veronica Roller," she said. "It would be my observation that Veronica Roller had some unsettled business from her days as a police officer, and it ended up getting her wife killed all these years later. Maybe. That could have been it, but I wasn't there, so I won't say firm. How does that sound to you?"

"What was the grudge and who held it?" I asked her.

"I imagine, that specifically who holds a grudge is a capital factor in what they do, don't do, or might still do about it. I don't know who it is in this case, if anyone, so I don't know why or if. And I didn't know Jessica personally and I don't know Veronica," Sandy said. "Just something or somebody from their past. In many ways there's nothing anybody can do about it now."

"Do you think it was all put to bed with Jessica's death, or is something still unresolved?" I asked her.

"I guess that depends on whether anyone still holds a grudge," she said. During our conversation we had traveled up to I-5, drove south for a few ramps, made a U-turn and returned again northward back to the industrial district where my car was parked at the Lickers' warehouse. She pulled back into the parking lot and dropped me off.

"Come see me anytime," she said. I walked to my car as she drove off. It was around five o'clock, it was still raining, and it was already

Denver Day

getting pretty dark in the Pacific Northwest. I drove back to the diner by the office to study the derby odds sheet while I ate my dinner. I phoned Tina on the way, to see whether she wanted to stop by for a bite before work.

The Davey Jones Lickers were clearly smiled upon by the oddsmakers. It was a good way to study up and fish around the circuit. I would need to request pin money from the department in order to place bets, though, having already spent a hundred bucks on this odds bill. My tofu scramble came about the same time that Tina showed up, soaking wet.

"It's really coming down out there, eh?" she said as she sat. She ordered the spaghetti. I showed her my sheet. "You want to get in on this? Our local Lickers are in the good graces of the bookmakers," I told her. She declined.

"I talked to the band, and we've counted our fair share of skate derby girls in and out of the club. But that's not particularly odd for any after-hours spot, or anywhere else for that matter, you know?" she said. "Nobody remembers seeing anything weird or particularly memorable along those lines, really. It's dark in there Rick, it is a jazz lounge you know, and don't forget that we're all musicians so we do our best to get over most any reasonable weirdness."

The lieutenant had already left for the day when I got back to the office, at about seven. I filled out reimbursement paperwork for funds to bet on the skater girls as part of my investigation. MacKinney would get a kick out of that. There was a message on my desk indicating that the Navajo DPS sergeant of detectives had returned my call.

Bill Moreno. I dialed that number back up, and got him on the line. As to be expected, Moreno said he'd already fielded several recent calls from various hats asking similar questions.

"Veronica grew up out here, her parents were school teachers at the Navajo Nation. She left our force about 10 years ago, and we hated to lose her. She was a competent officer and a good woman," Moreno said. "But, after she had to hook-up a close family friend for rape and murder, it ruined the appeal of the work for her, for good. She was ready to move away from here, and she left police work altogether."

"I had a girl up here today from within the ranks of the same derby league, speculating to me that the homicide of Veronica's girlfriend last week could be grounded to some aspect of her history at your agency," I told him.

"I'd say nothing specifically related to her police work. Of course you understand that some people take it personally when they get arrested, detective. Among many other duties and obligations, that's part of our job, and it was part of hers. Like I said, she was a great person to work with. Smart, fair and honest," Moreno said. "That particular case turned her taste for police work; it was tough on everybody. But there was nothing occult about it. No double-cross, no unresolved evidence, no second guessing or what-ifs. Very clear-cut, just one of those darker ones and it hit her too close to home. That was it for her. But I don't think there are any hot spots remaining."

"Makes perfect sense to me," I said.

On Wednesday morning, I arrived at work early again, and phoned Lopez first thing.

"Somebody needs to go to Arizona for an audience with Veronica Roller. I talked to the agency where she was formerly employed, and also talked to some of our local skate girls and one of them suggested Jessica's homicide might have roots somewhere in Veronica's past as a police officer," I briefed Lopez.

"A sergeant of detectives at the Navajo Nation said Veronica had to lock up a family friend, and that turned her off of police work forever. But, he believes that old story belongs in the past, and that it has no correlation with the Jessica Roller homicide. Moreover, I still haven't seen anything connecting Roller's homicide with any of Saturday's."

Lopez: "I talked to Moreno too, and got pretty much the same version as you. But along those lines, Veronica's perp in that case, who even today remains locked up in the ADC, well, his brother was the guy who Becca Roller, when she was Becca Reaugh, shot and killed in Scottsdale nine years ago. So there is a connection going back, between Becca and Veronica in that way. That's presumably how Veronica and Becca met. So a dead brother and a life sentence for yourself would be reason enough for some people to hold a grudge forever, against the household full of women who had been instrumental in bringing those circumstances about."

He made a good point, too. Lopez said the posties had also urged him to head out there to Phoenix, and that he'd already booked a flight.

Denver Day

Breaking News

When I got off the phone with Lopez, it was about ohh-six-hundred. I walked into the break room, reloaded the coffee pot and switched on the telly to the morning news. A reporter was standing on the shoulder of Harbor Bay Parkway in front of police tape, flashing lights, search and rescue vehicles, a media gang-bang with the San Francisco Bay in the background. It was still dark and the lights from all the fuzz at the scene jumped from the T.V. screen into our break room.

"I'm standing here about a mile north of Oakland International Airport, near the tragic scene where 20 women were found drowned about an hour ago, in an ambulance submerged in the San Francisco Bay. The vehicle apparently went in sometime late last night or early this morning. Eyewitnesses reported the situation to authorities," the reporter said. "Then came the search response."

"What sort of statements have been issued regarding the identity of those in the sunken vehicle? Has anyone commented regarding why so many people were in an ambulance?" the studio anchor questioned the on-scene reporter.

"The bodies have not all been positively identified, but they were reportedly all wearing the individually customized uniforms, to include roller skates, of Chino, California's Wheeled Beavers roller derby squad, when they were pulled from the water. Police stated that the team's entire roster may have been killed," the reporter replied.

"However, authorities have not commented as to why the women were in an ambulance in the first place, or regarding what they think may have caused the crash. But from the approximate location of the ambulance with respect to the nearest road, it was likely southbound on Harbor Bay Parkway when, for whatever reason, the driver failed to control the vehicle."

Holy hell, I thought to myself, the gals are really piling up out west this fall. I stood there for a minute, and got into the coffee. About that time, in came the lieutenant.

"According to this talking box, a whole squad of skater girls drowned in a crashed ambulance last night in the San Francisco Bay," I told him. "Your thoughts?"

"It wasn't me," he said. "Nobody's been able to link any derby girls to any dead strippers yet, anyway. We could just disregard causality in time and space entirely, and just plan on having a stripper blood bath one week, and a mass derby girl killing the next, and then alternating and repeating into forever for no good reason. But that is a cynical thing for me to say, and it also would look ridiculous in a police report, and it doesn't do much to keep the peace or serve and protect strippers or derby girls or hipsters or any other members of the general public."

Although he didn't seem to need it, he went

for the coffee too.

"Lopez out of San Diego is flying into Phoenix today, to get a face-to-face with Veronica and Becca Roller. I should call down right now to make sure he has a heads up for the people dealing with this drowned ambulance full of skater girls. And I'll head to our local Lickers warehouse today, to maybe see if anyone misses the now sunken Chino team or has anything to say about it. And to place a few bets, you want in on this action?" I smiled, waving the odds sheet at him.

"That's your department, wool rake," he said. "Meantime, I'll chat up the posties to the ambulance in the drink."

Meantime, I rang up the Alameda County Sheriff's Office, and brought their on-call duty officer and shift sergeant up to date on the 11 October homicides, the preceding Jessica Roller homicide in San Diego, and all the major relevant leads and ominous forensic alleys therewith. I listed for them the agencies so far involved, named the posties' liaison for the case, and sent them the cumulative inter-agency reports on the cases involving the strippers, as well as all the background information and rosters we had on the derby circuit. They said they'd be in touch along the way.

Despite the weirdness of their truck full of drowned skater ladies, the boys in Oakland were probably even more baffled after the conversation they had with me. Today had started out weird enough that the lieutenant had already locked himself in his office. I sent out a group memo addendum to the involved agencies about the latest fiasco in Oakland.

The guy who Becca Roller killed some decade ago was William Robert Crimson, who was 23 when he was shot to death during a domestic dispute with Becca (Reaugh) Roller. Crimson's older brother, who is still on the state farm in Arizona, is William Allan Crimson, now 48. He was convicted for rape and murder of a 16-year-old girl on the Navajo Nation.

Growing up, both the Crimson family and the victim's family were neighbors and friends of Veronica (Martinez) Roller's family. Veronica's mother taught all the Crimson children in school as well as all the kids from the victim's family. The trial was tragic enough, even before it was made furthermore disastrous by the national media.

Pizza Noir

Basically, Becca and Veronica and Jessica didn't meet one another until after all of that had happened. In fact, the unfortunate situation must have functioned as their introduction.

Granted, it was a little odd that the former Veronica Martinez ended up as the common law wife of the woman who killed the other Crimson brother. Anyway, it seems like Jessica just got rolled up in the middle of it, and from the pictures I've seen of her, she was the prettiest one of them all.

As Wednesday morning wrapped up, I headed back to the warehouse to place my bets and to commit the original sin of succumbing to the desire to spend more time with Sandy Licker. I got there about 12:30. There was a bit of a crowd as apparently was to be expected, judging by the looks of the scene. The squad was running line-on-line scrimmages. Two-minute runs each, which reflects the rules of the sport; two minutes per line shift and scoring opportunity, with two thirty minute rounds comprising a match.

I saw the guys who had given me the odds sheet the day before, sitting in the same huddle, watching the girls go around. I put fifty bucks on the Lickers for Saturday's match, and another fifty on them to win again the following week.

Sandy was a defensive player, a blocker. Two of the guys making books had Russian accents, which seems like not a totally unusual accent for bookmakers. I thought it was pretty auspicious in light of our unidentified dead guy in the Russian suit, although for all we may ever know, that dude was as American as apple pie and had simply come across a good bargain on a foreign suit in his size. I emboldened the mental note just in case: Add Russian bookmakers to this bubbling rock-and-roll stew of strippers, pizza men, and skaters.

At about 2 o'clock, they broke up the scrimmage. I wheeled myself down there and greeted Sandy. I told her the news about the Chino team.

"Weird. You know, that was their own ambulance. I believe they got a pretty good deal on it, and it was big enough to fit their whole squad into," she said.

"Besides the obvious general tragedy of it, it's tough for the circuit to lose a whole squad. You get to know the smell and the smiles and the glares and the snarls of your competitors. It's like puppy love, and there's great respect among athletes. Chivalry truly." She pouted and wiped away a tear.

"Wanna go for another ride?" she asked.

"Absolutely," I replied.

She unstrapped her skates, laced up her high tops, grabbed her bag, and we headed out to the parking lot. "I'll drive again," she said.

Again she grabbed us two cold ones from the cooler in the backseat and we pulled out of the parking lot. About ten minutes later we arrived at her apartment. Her quarters were like a tiny museum and a customized tree house all rolled into one. There was a bicycle strung up from the ceiling, and a few hammocks and some hanging chairs on chains.

The walls were fully coated with a mosaic of articles, paintings, collages, drawings, photographs, and the shelves were filled with books, this-and-that origami everything, knickknacks, bowls and vases, figurines, fishbowls, rocks, incense, and crystals. The place was verily alive with stuff crammed from corner to corner to corner to corner to corner to corner.

There was a kitchenette to the left of the door and a pillow-filled niche behind a curtain of beads. We walked through the wall of beads and she lowered the light. She kissed me, ordered me bare, removed her uniform and blew my mind. Ninety minutes later she returned me to my car as if coughing up a hairball.

Lopez got off the plane at Phoenix Sky Harbor International Airport, rented a sedan and booked a room at a hotel near the airport. He dropped off his carry-on bag in his room, and looked at the north Phoenix address he'd been given by the MCSO. He drove to the sheriff's office and met with some of the detectives there for about thirty minutes, then headed north on I-17 for about ten more.

It was about 2:45 p.m. when he knocked on the Rollers' apartment door. He'd told them to expect him about 3 o'clock. Becca answered the door wearing the Rollers' baby blue standard. She and Veronica had just returned from a scrimmage. She invited him in. Veronica made tea. Becca was muscular and not very tall, but she was attractive, and had beautiful green eyes.

Veronica had already changed out of her uniform into jeans and a plain cotton t-shirt. She was tall with steely blue eyes, although she had a subtle and disarming smile. They sat him down at the kitchen table.

Lopez looked at the stainless steel teapot. Becca ducked out and came back having quickly showered and changed into plainclothes. The three sat and talked for about an hour.

"I loved Jessica, we both did. She was our partner. Understand that you're talking with her two grieving and recently bereft sisters, detective," Veronica said. He nodded.

"Becca and I met during the Crimson murder trial. A short time later, she shot Bobby Crimson during some heavily intoxicated argument, and then went to ADC for 18 months," Veronica said. "In the meantime, I quit the Navajo force and moved out here to Phoenix. When Becca was paroled, she moved in with me and a few years later we met Jessica through the derby circuit. We fell in love with her. She moved in with us five years ago."

She continued: "But I keep in touch with Allan Crimson. In the last decade, the Crimson and Martinez families have remained in contact and we visit on holidays. One must hold on to the good of what you had and still have or else you have nothing left at all. So, Allan Crimson didn't have, he would never have, anything to do with

Denver Day

this. Nobody conjured this up, Jessica's death came by a random barfight dust-up, a crime of dull passion in a meaningless jackass hash. In one slip. I was there, it was too perfectly stupid to be premeditated or to end well."

A Simple Task

I sat there in my car, smoking.

I had asked Sandy about the Russian bookmakers. She said they were just part of the scenery, and, that anyway, it was only natural for people to enjoy betting on fastly round-and-round-rolling pretties.

I'd told her that one of our two 11 October dead dudes had a tailor-made Russian suit on, carried no identification, and no one had yet claimed his body. And, I mentioned that, maybe, she'd bring it up to some of the Russian wallflowers hanging about the Lickers' warehouse, as that might inspire somebody to mosey in to the morgue and claim a comrade. It was about 4 when I got back to the office.

"You have a certain air about you, Ricky," MacKinney quipped. "By the way, Dixie called. And Oakland wants you to ring them back, too, they said just whenever you get a moment."

So, I dialed up Dixie first.

"I finally had a call about an hour ago, on the dude in the suit. And the person on the line did have an English-as-a-second-language, European- sounding accent. A man. He said he'd

Denver Day

be around in the next couple of days to attempt to identify and possibly claim our Euro. He didn't say any names or any relationship to the deceased. He didn't say when exactly he'd come, and he hasn't been here yet," she said.

"I'll stay nearby. Call me the instant anyone shows up," I said.

I told her the bookmakers for our town's Davey Jones Lickers were Russians, and by-the-way a whole team of derby girls had crashed their ambulance into the San Francisco Bay last night, all drowned.

"Keep that in mind, for what it's worth," I said.

"Yeah right Rick," Dixie answered.

I rang up Oakland next, and those boys had a fucking DOOZEY. I don't know what else to call it.

Chief Detective Sam Wilson of the Oakland PD: "I really don't know how to explain. I feel funny putting it into words, detective, so I'll just say it. You know we pulled all those dead girls out of the drink this morning, and, well, one of them, the one in the driver seat, was all furry. Allover."

What did he mean "all furry," I wondered.

"What do you mean 'all furry'?" I asked.

Pizza Noir

"I mean all five-foot-four of her is fucking furry with furry fur. And with dog's teeth, paws, and eight nipples. Pointy ears. The whole schmeer," Wilson said. "She was wearing the Chino Beavers uniform with the nickname FirePie stitched profusely into her skirts, but I can think of more appropriate nicknames for her after seeing what I saw this morning. Our coroner, quite frankly, is completely mystified."

I could certainly understand his frustration. It was quite a story.

Several Alameda County Coroners Office staff, several deputies, the medics, and the city police who came in with the drowned women all stared at the furry oddity on the autopsy table in front of them with great curiosity, prolonged disbelief and general astonishment. The hair looked coarse, but it was soft to the touch.

They had removed the uniform she'd drowned in, a black and pink miniskirt and a black and white plaid sports-support tank top. Her matching canvas high tops sat on the lab table next to her uniform. Her 19 teammates were bagged up in there also, but this surprise from nature was, not surprisingly, getting all the attention.

Like a felled moose, her tongue lolled out of her mouth, and trails of saltwater and saliva darkened the fur on her cheeks.

"She's beautiful," the assistant coroner mooned. "Look at those native female features. That soft, shiny coat."

Standing next to the assistant coroner, one of his colleagues was chomping at the bit to get the autopsy underway, curious of her innards. Eyes wide, they all looked on.

But when their guy put a scalpel to her torso, the corpse shuddered. The instinctive response of all who were standing around the table was to jump backwards several feet. Except for the coroner's staffer who made the incision.

His instinct was to bleed to death. He couldn't jump, because his neck was in her mouth and she was fanning her head back and forth with gurgling bloody hydraulic violence. A fine misty spray of blood gradually darkened the walls and the surfaces of pretty much everything in the room like a coat of spray paint, as she rigorously and rhythmically shook her mouthful back and forth.

She was also sucking as she shook her

head, and the foamy squelch of that was very audible to the others in the room above the freaky growls coming from the monster's own rotten bowels. She drank his blood his blood straight from the tap as she murdered him up. When her breakfast was finally all spazzed out, and his juices were mostly every where but inside of him, she dropped the body, moved toward the bloodied door, and walked out.

The men in the room stood there for several long moments, covered in the blood of their late associate, and all looking rather blankly at the door through which had just exited the portent object of her victim's forensic exam, which had gotten more out of hand than any such alike throughout the entire history of autopsies.

When Lopez came away from his afternoon with Veronica and Becca Roller, he had a clear intuition that the women were telling the frank truth as they understood it. He found their judgments about the Crimson issue to be well-corroborated by facts and nature and sociology. About the time he got back to his hotel, he took a call from me.

"These girls out here are pretty much big

teddy bears. In all likelihood, there's more to them than would be fit to pin as suspects in the October 11 homicides. And Veronica Roller's historical account of the relationship between hers and the Crimson family also shows a cool forensic trail," Lopez said. "Institutionally, I think we can still look at the derby circuit, but individually, these girls have honest accounts and are likely clean."

"Did they look wolfy at all?" I asked him.

"I'm sorry did you say wolfy?" he asked back.

"Lopez, 'something of interest' happened last night in Oakland. To say the least. Then, later this afternoon, something TOTALLY APESHIT has occurred down there for their follow-up act. Although how this pertains to the price of tea in China or to the October 11 homicides still isn't clear," I said.

"So go ahead," Lopez said.

"OPD fished the entire Chino Beavers derby squad out of the drink in the San Francisco Bay. They crashed their ambulance in there last night and all drowned," I said. "All of them."

"Hmmm," he said.

"Yes hmmm. But apparently the driver had

some anomalous characteristics," I said.

"Oh? Like what?" he asked.

"She was a woman-sized canine-like creature in a Chino Wheeled Beavers uniform," I said. "No shit, so they tell me. A werewolf lady, but that's not all. When they put the blade to her in a forensic exam, or rather when they tried to, she shot up off the table and ate one of the Alameda County coroner's staff. And then she, it, whatever, simply hot-footed right on out the door."

"Well, I can tell you that these Phoenix girls appeared to be slick bodied creatures, Rick. They did not come across as nascent werewolves. Then again, I don't know what the early warning signs for that sort of thing would be, or what's the difference. Anyway, I wasn't looking for B-movie monsters," he said. "Did anyone shoot at her when she ran off?"

"Good question. Probably. I don't know. But she lived through drowning, so we don't know how many lives these things have, but it's clearly more than just one," I said. "And, apparently, there is one on the loose in Oakland, for whatever that fact may be worth to the likes of us in Tacoma or in San Diego."

The aftermath of Wednesday afternoon's

Denver Day

Oakland incident involved a good number of people standing around looking confused. And, in fact, everyone with a firearm indeed had unloaded into the freak as she was headed for the door, if not while she was still eating the coroner's assistant. So that made it easier to track her because she was pretty drippy.

They trailed her about a half mile south of the coroners office, where it looked as if she'd jumped into Oakland Inner Harbor waterway. Authorities down there dived and dragged all that night, fruitlessly. They did their best to mop up all the gore from their morgue, and preserve the peace while it might last, if possible.

But I could understand their plight. It's difficult to write down or say "werewolf" or "moon dog" and expect it to satisfy bereaved family members or anyone else, even if it's not in an official report. By now, Oakland was glad to have the posties come out to lift a leg on their fireplugs, since the only story OPD had, and the facts as they understood them were not whatsoever believable.

However, let it be said and let it be known that timing related to suspension of disbelief is a critical forensic parameter. Up here in Tacoma, the sun went down and the rain continued. At the diner, I sat with hot coffee, doodled on my napkin, and glanced around the room from time to time. I made small talk with the waitress when she came and went by. After getting that weird-assed story from Oakland, the lieutenant and I had just called it a day. It was technically quitting time anyway.

People seem to be repeating this often, but I'll say it again. Sometimes goofy odd stuff happens and all police, medics, and first responders among others, as a general group will agree. Stuff that just doesn't make sense and may not ever un-kink. Often you sense it right when you step in it, in whatever form it arrives.

Still, just like things that are immediately explainable, the confusing stuff still burns an image, a memory in the mind's eye. So you get into a sort of habit of taking everything in stride so you can still work, regardless of circumstance or sensory input, explainable or not.

Frequently, we're thrust into situations that are undefined, at least temporarily, but they must nevertheless be navigated regardless of how inconvenient and queer they are or seem to be. The waitress navigated over to me and topped off my coffee with a smile.

Denver Day

I didn't know what we were expected to do about the weird story from Oakland. Hell, they had no idea what to think either. I felt sorry for those boys down there having to deal with no less than the supernatural.

More importantly, nobody had drawn any hard connection between the derby circuit and the October 11 killings. So, supernatural or not, as far as anyone knew, Oakland's new oddity was as irrelevant to our investigation as it was fishy. The important correlation among all the events was their incoherence, and nobody had explained any of it. Random. Unrelated but for etherial, circumstantial, quazi-relationships.

At about eight, I went home to take it easy more. I sat around the apartment in my boxers, clicking one of my revolvers at the screen while I watched old black and white crime drama. I grew bored of that and switched it over to newer, in-color crime drama. I wrote in my journal, about the events of the day and the developments in the caseload. Getting thoughts out on paper sometimes helps me find new perspective for the loose ends, mysteries, and clouded issues of the week. Somewhere along the way, I dozed off on the couch. About 1:30 in the morning, the phone rang. It was Dixie.

"Get your narrow ass down to the morgue. A.S.A.P.," she demanded.

"OK. Put on some coffee, I'll be there directly," I answered. I grabbed a clean white shirt, replaced my pants and coat, and struck out into the rain on an early Thursday morning.

Out Through the In Door

When I got there, a few Pierce County Sheriff's Office vehicles were in the coroner's office parking lot. Deputies were dusting about the doors and creating paperwork.

"We are missing several pieces of your evidence," she said.

I didn't like what I thought she was about to say, but she said it anyway.

"So. All three of your October 11 bodies are gone. The building's security alarms went off about 0100. I don't know what else the deputies have found so far, but one of the docks in the back was wide open."

"Were the security cameras rolling?" I asked.

"Yep. The boys are in there looking at the tape right now," she said.

Dixie and I walked around back, where on the east side of the building there are two vertical-door vehicle docks. The north door was all the way open. More rain fell. We went back inside. In one of the supply closets was the digital surveillance system monitor, and one of the county investigators was eyeballing the tape. He backed up the grainy black-and-white recording for us.

"You can see the glow of head-lights here, in the parking lot to the east. They're approaching from the north, at about time-stamp 0058. A sedan of some kind, as you can see here where the vehicle's cab doesn't protrude above the hedges and landscaping between this lot and the one behind us, to the east."

"The vehicle pulls around 180 degrees and stops, but the headlights stay on. There's no audio on the tape, but the assumption is that the vehicle was left running. Then, from through the hedge comes this individual, jogging across the parking lot, in a long coat."

"You can't make out facial features because of the shadows and rain, but he or she here gives one yank on the garage door and throws it open. It comes right up. There are no cameras inside the office, so the next time we see this person is at time-stamp 0101, coming back through the open garage door, carrying what appears to be your three bodies, the biggest on the bottom, and looks like probably the girl on top. Like pancakes!"

"Through the hedge and quickly you see the glow of vehicle lights as the car's put back into gear and starts back north," the deputy said.

"Looks like they just walked in, picked up who they needed from the body locker, and moseyed right out. Why was the door unlocked?" I asked.

"Shouldn't have been, and it wasn't when I left," Dixie answered. "Those docks are where we take in shipments from medical trucks and slow-rolling ambulances, and we load up the out-bound funeral wagons through those doors too. Those back doors were last used late yesterday afternoon, and I double-checked them myself before I cleared out of here for the day at about seven."

"When any of the family members ask, I'll just tell them that they have to keep waiting because the case remains open and sensitive. But that story won't last forever. Eventually, I think the girl's family would litigate if we didn't hand her over. Maybe not the others."

"But it's a fact that right now the bodies are gone, and very possibly gone forever. I don't know what to tell you," Dixie said.

She made a good point. Where to look. The nearest sausage factory? A taxidermist?

"Dixie I might speculate, this was the visit

yesterday promised to you by the guy with the Russian accent on the phone," I said, "in which case, he's really gone the extra mile."

Since I was already up and about, I drove through the rain down the I-5, to the Lickers' warehouse. I figured I could take a look at the parking lot in the hours after the body snatchings to make note of the vehicles, but the place was barren. Not tonight, honey. I pulled into the lot and circled the warehouse, got back onto the freeway, and headed north.

About 10 minutes later I approached Sandy's apartment complex, which was glowing like the center of the sun, with an aroma of smoky contraband and the ambiance of loud music. But it was their crowd, not college kids. I kind of felt like an asshole because she knew I was a cop, and a connection by association through her was the only lead anybody had, so far, on the disappeared bodies. And hell, for all I knew, she was a werewolf too, and if that, then why not the whole lot of them?

I am getting too old for this, I mumbled to myself. Anyway, whatever. Here I was. I could get a good look at the nightlife, have a beer, and find out what the good word was this morning from the derby.

There was a covered open-air common courtyard area with a running wet bar and several kegs tapped, but whoever had been staffing that drink service, if anyone, had wandered off. Some people chatted here and there in the corners, but I didn't immediately see Sandy. Seemed like most everybody had receded from the wet outdoor air to the tables, living rooms, and kitchens of the town homes, many of whose doors were cracked, from which various sounds and scents drifted. I walked behind the bar and grabbed a yellow can of lager from the ice well, cracked it open and leaned on the bar.

There was a kind of nostalgic feeling that wafted up from my younger days, when I kept these same hours and ran in circles like this. The cold lager warmed the clammy autumn air quite a bit. One of the women walked up and dug a beer out of the same ice chest.

"Hello detective," she brooded. "Sandy's around, she's probably over at her place."

"Thank you. You guys celebrating something?" I asked her.

"Samhain. A little early this year, but the

new moon's tonight," she said.

She asked for a cigarette which I rendered. She put it to her lips, I put a match to it and asked what her position was.

"A jammer. My name's Kitty Licker and it's nice to meet you," Kitty curtsied. "We've got a home match Saturday. You coming?"

"I wouldn't miss it," I said.

She smiled. We chatted; she gave me a partial tour of her tattoos. We finished our beers, and walked together toward Sandy's flat. Sandy and a half dozen others were sitting around in her dwarvish ontological-museum-like dwelling; playing cards, smoking and joking. A twangy record orbited the turntable pin. Sandy stood and greeted me with a hug and kiss on both cheeks.

The Licker's jammer who'd walked me in sat down next to a guy who handed her the unplugged Stratocaster he'd been tinkering with. Sandy turned over the record, then she and I went and stood together in the kitchenette area. I asked her to elaborate to me about the bookmakers I'd met at the Lickers' warehouse.

"Kinda shady European dudes, and they rotate in and out on their own dime. They don't really socialize with us as such, and I don't gamble on the circuit or on anything, so I and the girls don't interact much with them. But people like them do serve a purpose, not the least of which is to make books on our derby," Sandy said. "As you suggested today, I mentioned to one of them that the cops had an unclaimed Russian stiffy at the county morgue. He just handed me a complimentary odds sheet, and went about his business scribbling on a notebook and yakking with his associates."

"Generally, those boys add to the carnival flavor of the scene, and they don't bother anyone anyway. There are a lot of other interesting characters who hang around besides them," she said.

"Oh, it's flavorful," I said. "Speaking of which, thank you for the ride today."

She smiled. "Anytime. How's the case otherwise?"

I told her we'd had our first contact of any sort regarding the unidentified guy in the suit, on the previous afternoon, and that something about that had led me to believe there might be a connection between local bookmakers and local drug dealers, irrelevant as it may be to the killings.

"Well, you gotta admit that isn't much of a shocker," she said.

"What's more, though, is that the unidentified body and the other two victims in the case were all three stolen from the morgue a couple of hours ago," I explained. "I didn't know what else to do besides come out for a beer to clear my head."

I watched her thinking about her response. Stolen dead people is not boring conversation material.

"Wow. Body snatchers, eh? Wasn't me," she winked. "But I can see why you draw a possible connection with the bookmakers."

"Also, something weird as a Chinese sandwich has come up out of Oakland, about the demise of the Chino Beavers," I added.

"Oh friend, pray do tell?" she asked.

"The driver, by the derby name of FirePie Beaver, in her death had apparently turned into some sort of wolf lady, they discovered upon fishing her from the bay," I explained.

"Then, when they put the blade to her at the coroner's office, she quickened, eviscerated the man with the scalpel, and ran off. They all unloaded on her, but she kept right on running,

Denver Day

jumped into the Oakland Inner Harbor about a mile away, and disappeared. This was yesterday afternoon. As I mentioned, the three bodies disappeared this morning."

She responded with a flash of disbelief, followed by a cool quiet.

"I've said this to you before. Sometimes things happen Rick that don't make logical sense. I would qualify this matter as such a thing," she said. "Especially now, and you had better start getting used to it. And I don't have your bodies so let's go to bed."

She gave a wave to her buddies, who cleared out of the apartment and shut the door behind them. I woke up about 5 o'clock at Sandy's, probably about thirty minutes or an hour after I'd fallen asleep, to the sound of the tinny, high-pitched alarm on my digital wristwatch. Sandy was already not there. I could hear rain outside. I used her restroom and, for the second time that morning I replaced my trousers, shirt, shoes, and coat.

I let myself out. The party was over, the courtyard was dark, the complex had finally gone to sleep. Not a peep and not a person but for the who's who always of the rain. The bar still stood open, vacant, and dark but still iced and stocked. It was drizzling heavily. Between the new moon and the loud cover it was pitch dark but for whatever electric lighting came and went. I walked to the lot, keyed into my car and sat down, cranked the motor and drove toward the street.

As I pulled onto the thoroughfare and began to accelerate, I glanced into the rear view mirror and saw two figures standing at the corner of the parking lot I'd just exited. I quickly looked again, braking to light up the path behind me, but then there was nothing. Just rain. The temperature of my hair, skin, and teeth took a little dive.

I knew I could lock the brakes, turn around right bloody then and troll that parking lot, until the sun came up and the rain stopped, and wouldn't see a soul. It was a pretty drafty ride to breakfast.

Denver Day

A Desert of Answers

I was a little wet, dizzy, and rumpled, so I made directly for Joe's coffee to address my improving condition. He was standing under the awning of his kiosk, peering into the precipitation, although visibility seemed only about two feet, no matter who you were or in what direction you looked.

The weather was going a long way toward giving everything a nice, cozy, self-effacing coat this week. A natural aid to forgetting one's troubles. We stood there together, looking into the soup, having some nice hot brown caffeinated water.

"Boy how, you do look like hell," he said.

One of the newspapers at Joe's stand had a below-the-fold headline about the Chino Beaver's watery demise, but the copy didn't include any mention of the mystery surrounding their driver, the late and former FirePie Beaver, nor of her autopsy fiasco:

Oakland, Calif. (AP)—The entire Chino Wheeled Beavers roller derby squad drowned in the San Francisco Bay early Wednesday.

Denver Day

The team used an ambulance for transportation to competitions, and its driver apparently lost control of the vehicle as it traveled south on Harbor Bay Parkway. It crashed into the water about a mile north of the Oakland International Airport . . . .

"This, Joe," I said, "isn't the half of it." I told him the tall tale parlayed to us by the OPD on the previous afternoon. He showed no pity. "Water, water everywhere," he taunted.

"There's more, coffeeman," I said, taking a slurp. "Our three bodies disappeared from the morgue very early this morning, and the only connecting lead we have, tenuous as it is, possibly links that morgue robbery, and in particular the unidentified Russian dead guy, with some foreign national freelancers who run numbers on the local derby squad, that is, our own lovely and local Davey Jones Lickers. Likely a dead end but it's the only theory which doesn't involve the supernatural.

He laughed at me, and at the natural irony of the situation. Low-hanging fruit.

"Water, water, everywhere, and monsters ate your only evidence," he chimed.

Pizza Noir

His busting my balls didn't stop the rain, but it did lighten me up a little on what had already been a long Thursday morning. And, because of the weather conditions, it was still pre-dawn, in effect.

About the same time down in Oakland, Alameda County Coroner's Office staff arrived to find the rest of the Chino girls disappeared from their deep freeze. Now, of course, it was anybody's ball game.

Local search and rescue responders had been dragging and diving the Oakland Inner Harbor since the wolverized FirePie Beaver jumped in it Thursday. They kept it up all day, but without any luck at all. Not a stitch.

Unlike the incident up here in Pierce County, the Alameda County Coroner didn't have surveillance footage, because their closed circuit camera system had been damaged during the autopsy incident Wednesday, and the system was still down when the rest of the Chino girls disappeared from the morgue. Communiqués circulated among police agencies, particularly those involved in the October 11 homicide investigations, urging ratcheted-up security at the respective coroners' facilities. Lock up your dead.

Denver Day

For once he was glad to see the posties, OPD Chief Detective Sam Wilson thought to himself, as he read through the brave attempts at logical reports which had been submitted by those present at FirePie's autopsy and the aftermath.

Usually, when the feds help, there is a carrot and a stick. The carrot is toys for local agencies, and the stick is a perceived risk to autonomy in a given local jurisdiction.

In this case it did not matter, Wilson thought, and he welcomed any investigative insight. God knows what might be coming next; we're peace officers, not interstellar mutant bounty hunters, Wilson thought. In this case, he needed a third party institution to bear witness, help document the strange events, and bring his department above any suspicion of having made the whole GDF'n thing up.

Meanwhile, from nearly 6 in the morning on, nobody had seen yesterday's morgue escapee, and nobody had seen last night's morgue disappearees either.

There were no signs of forced entry. Only the front door left quaintly unlocked for the first shift to discover when they arrived, apparently having been the egress used for the Chino Beavers' unexpected emancipation.

The body of the county employee killed by FirePie was also gone from the morgue, for better or worse.

The press had not caught wind of the seemingly supernatural aspects of the case, and as far as Wilson or anybody else was concerned, they didn't need to.

When Lopez's returning red eye arrived at San Diego International, he switched on his mobile phone to find a message from Veronica Roller: "Hey Lopez, Veronica here. Call me when you get this." He promptly did so.

"Yes ma'am?" he asked when she picked up.

"I understand there was a more or less unexplainable thing that happened in Oakland yesterday," Veronica said. "I just wanted to tell you, that word got out here, about what happened with FirePie Beaver yesterday afternoon out west. And I want to tell you that, back home at the Navajo Nation, there are legends or historical folklore about things like this."

Denver Day

"What happened in Oakland is not based on reading, writing or arithmetic. It has to do with the neverending relationships between the earth and those who walk upon it, and the cycles of birth, life, and death, the moon and stars. Anyway, hope that helps. We'll be listening and learning what we can from our position, and we are thinking about paying you a visit sometime in the near future."

Lopez begged the question, nearing frustration: "Veronica, there's the general supposition that yesterday's incidents up in Oakland are somehow connected to the October 11 killings because of the inter-relationships, vague as the are, between the derby and the bookmakers for Tacoma's Davey Jones Lickers. Even more nebulous are the connections between the burglary of the Pierce County morgue, and the metastasizing mess down at the coroner in Alameda County. If this was at all somehow looped back into the bar fight you guys were involved with, in the week before all this started, it would seem to be connected in name or style only, so to speak. Just because there's a connection doesn't mean it's part of the problem."

"Are you telling me that you've actually seen

instances of this sort of human-canine thing? Or are you just saying these cases can't be resolved with secular police work? We have zero arrests. Zero suspects. Even if anyone had a clue, how in the hell is anybody supposed to prosecute real, live, literal monsters? Or the dead? Or dead monsters?' Lopez ranted.

"Exactly, Joe. And I'm saying there are ancient folkways and realities that may not come up in any court or grand jury, yet they exist. They're out there, and sometimes the right fates cross, and the circumstances allow for them to manifest, after a fashion that makes them as real as they are old," Veronica said. "So, you're right. There's a certain threshold beyond which police jurisdiction as you know it is irrelevant. But I can help. Keep in touch. This too shall pass."

When I shined into the office, minimally revitalized by the effects of Joe's coffee, it was still dark, but my message board was glowing like a yule log.

First a note from MacKinney, who said he had several messages from the Seattle Bureau Chief Hays, who reported having several urgent requests from national headquarters regarding a newfound interest in our case by other posties. Because of the potential international nature of the case now stemming from the potential involvement of European bookmakers, additional Alphabet Soup was now upon us.

Good luck, I thought, and probably channeled a little of Detective Wilson's sentiment up from Oakland. Inasmuch as they could explain away werewolves (and they might, you never know), the posties could be of pivotal relevance. The development would certainly help in organizational oversight, and providing general sunlight for the increasingly myopic investigation.

I debriefed some alphabet man in D.C. by phone; regarding the bookies and their accents, and the dead guy in the В. Конычу suit, and the suspicious phone call Dixie received after I had mentioned the unclaimed body to the Lickers' squad captain; and the subsequent disappearance from our morgue of the three dead whose original demise was syncopated with the other 11 October homicides; and the possible link to a deadly San Diego bar fight involving the Phoenix Bloody Rollers two weeks prior. I explained about the Chino Beavers' watery demise and the late events in Oakland including their freaky autopsy.

"But on that topic, I couldn't tell you anymore," I said. "And I don't think Oakland could tell you much more than that either, at this point."

"You look like hell Rick, damn. Go back home and go to bed," MacKinney declared when he arrived at the office.

"Well, I tried to turn in early last night, but the fates had something else in mind for me," I replied. Anyway, I took his suggestion to heart.

"Thanks Mac. I'll be back this afternoon." Out the door I went, day sleeper for the day, hopefully.

Denver Day

Eye of the Storm

When I got back to the office about 4 o'clock that afternoon, there were yet more messages, as well as an attractive alphabet postie waiting for me. She had a qualitative lecture for me about who did and who didn't, by her standards, qualify as a member of the Russian mafia.

"Basically, your guys running books for the derby team are young, second-generation, former-Eastern-Bloc ex-pats. In the sense that they are Russian, and that their racket is organized, and paper related, well, then what they're doing can be categorized as ancillary to an organized, white-collar, ethnic-Russian syndicate."

"But. It's decentralized. They're not tipping out upward through any command chain, because they don't have one, inasmuch as they don't answer to any person or group overseas or anywhere else."

"So they're actually just local businessmen. Legal eagles. Basically just American emigres running books. More specifically, they're citizens of the great state of Washington, and as far as I know, there aren't any rules up here prohibiting

Denver Day

reasonable gambling in good faith. Or are there?"

"Anyway, they're all yours, detective," she continued. "But I'll say that body theft, as from your morgue yesterday and from Alameda County's last night, is something that we can't pin to any organized crime trend or any trend otherwise. As you would presume, that type of crime connotes typically not a group dynamic profile; but rather individual operators. Like morticians, for example. Or organ traffickers. Time was, for the common criminal, cadavers were only useful for necrophilia, or luggage, or science. Alas, times have changed."

A lovely alphabet soup lady with a sense of humor.

"However," she pressed, returning to her serious face. "Regarding this business down in Oakland with what they dragged out of the bay? We don't suggest silver bullets, but high caliber-high velocity ammunition is recommended," she laughed again.

"Hollow points, babe. Seriously be careful. You guys out here might, as precautionary measures, ramp up your presence and your fire-power at places like naked-lady bars, roller derby events, and your coroners' facilities. I suggest you send out a group advisory to all of the agencies involved, saying just as much. All just in case. Precautionary measures."

"And you might check with your wardens and jailers and quartermasters, asking after odd behavior among inmates and animals. Sometimes a little weirdness among certain populations coincides with increased trends in supernatural activities. You know."

So there I had it right from the horse's mouth. Even though our morgue and Alameda County's were already emptied out, the idea of putting units armed for bear guarding the doors around the clock seemed to be sage advice, which I promptly passed along to the relevant agencies.

It may have been futile, but it gave some sense of comfort. Shotguns have that effect. Through the rest of the afternoon, as the rain outside kept up; I remained at the office having phone conversations with my colleagues up and down the coast, comparing stories.

Lopez also spent much of his day on the phone and was met with several memos, one of which by way of me from the posties strongly suggested that he put bigger guns at important doors. He had slept a little on the plane, and had come into his office that morning right after he dropped off his bags at his apartment and showered, and shaved.

Lopez put in a call back to Maricopa County and the Phoenix PD, since he was the one primarily communicating with the Arizona contacts, in order to deliver the newest inter-agency advisories.

Before he left his office for the afternoon, Lopez called back to the household of Veronica and Becca Roller for another convo, but this time nobody picked up, as those girls had slipped off the map for a while.

Meanwhile, I cleared out of my office about seven, ate dinner at the diner, and drove over to MCs to see who I might see. It was a warm relief to be among the Thursday evening crowd and out of the rain. I didn't see Alvarez in there, but I recognized a couple of the waitresses as off-duty Tacoma Lickers, particularly my new friend Kitty Licker, whose MCs Ale House uniform looked a lot the same as her derby rigging, but for this gig she wore black canvas high tops instead of skates.

Note to self, I thought; gotta keep an eye

out for Eastern Block suits and bookmakers in here too. I sat at the bar, but Kitty diverted my business from the barkeep. She brought me a neat single malt and one for herself which she sipped.

"I'll be right back," she said. The whiskey was warm in my belly, and there was good hockey on the telly. Soon returned Kitty, who finished off her glass and asked for my card, which I gave her. Then she asked me to write the address of my apartment on the back, which I did.

"I'll be over this morning about one. Your drink's on the house." She turned on her heel and walked off.

I didn't recognize tonight's bartender or any of the patrons. I finished my glass and headed out. I drove over to the Diddler, and as the clock crowded eight, a healthy Thursday evening crowd was accumulating. The stripper pier was lit up and the music was cranked.

A blonde wearing a pink thong and feathered, high-laced strappy sandals spun around on one of the poles until she about fucked it. She had the same ivy tramp stamp as the lady missing from our morgue. In fact, she appeared similarly tattooed in all the same places, from where I sat. She finished her act, and disappeared into the trap door in the stripper pier.

Next came a double act, a gothic bit with both girls in black lace and raven hair, black vinyl collars, pointy black boots, black lipstick, and all. They also had a go at the poles, then at each other, which very much pleased the crowd.

To both the blonde and the gothic duo, I included my business card folded into the tips that I slid into their garments, as a sort of fishing expedition. The girls knew who I was by now; so if they were tempted to give the police any color analysis on the ever-cooling 11 October cases, or whatever else, they'd have the right contact information.

I went from there to the Squeeze Box, as it was getting to about 10 o'clock. It was a pretty lively scene, too. The redheaded act who had been wearing baby blue here during a recent visit was up there again. This time she was wearing a very few green sequins, possibly as few as five or ten. Or maybe the stage lights were just green, and she was naked except for some glitter and a hat.   I tipped her a business card wrapped in two Jackson notes, and sat down at the bar. I looked down to the end of it, and there was Keri Anders and Louis Ho. I waved. They sent me a pint of stout, then soon moved down to join me.

"Thanks for the beer," I said. "You kids doing OK?"

Ho nodded and grunted in the affirmative, yeah.

"I'm doing better Ricky. I've been born again," Keri answered.

She looked normal for her, although she did have a new fever blister. She took a drag on her menthol, took a pull from her highball, and blew smoke toward my ear. Moving ahead with my fishing expedition, I told them the three bodies had all been stolen from the morgue, and that there had been such a pilfering down in Oakland too.

"Nooooooo shit. I told you this whole deal was haunted. I suspected vampires, but hearing this? Now I say zombies. We'll let you know if we see them, Ricky," she dutifully answered. "Oh shit, I'm due backstage."

With that, they both stood up, Ho headed out the front door, uh-huh, and Anders headed toward the back of the house. I watched a couple more acts, tipped my requisite cards and cash to each, including Anders. En route home, I stopped

Denver Day

back through the diner for coffees and caught up with the past several days' worth of newspapers.

About fifteen minutes after I got home, Kitty walked in with a six pack, which ended in a 3-3 tie after a giggly hour of cigarettes and late night T.V. Unlike her teammate, Kitty didn't disappear from the bed in the night, so she was still there when my phone woke us up at about 6. It was Wilson out of Oakland again.

"Ahh, Thompson?"

"Speaking," I answered.

"It's Sam Wilson again, down in Oakland. All agencies are in as of about ten minutes ago. All the 11 October bodies are gone now. Every town, every damn one of them," he said. "And naturally nobody saw nothing."

Oof. Extra innings.

"OK. Thanks for the heads up. I'll catch up with you later this morning," I said. I hung up the phone, and snuggled with Kitty.

The Magic Number

We woke up again about eight. I figured there was no rush to chase dead people, at least not before I got a little more much-needed sleep. Kitty put on a pair of my sweatpants and an old shirt, I took a shower and we left about 8:30.

"I'll say hi to Sandy for you. See you Saturday night."

I telephoned MacKinney. "I heard from Oakland about two and half hours ago. You got anything?"

"Just that all the October 11 bodies are gone from everywhere. I heard every agency involved, uniformly no witnesses, and a complete lack of good surveillance footage either due to incidental system malfunction or blocked cameras. I heard any extra guards posted last night were circumvented, whether on a coffee break, or off taking a piss, or were just flat-out catburgled flat footed. I heard no signs of forced entry anywhere either, Rick, like those gals just got up and hoofed it."

"What's your game plan?" I asked.

"Stick with the Lickers and keep an eye on their bookies," he said. "Mind your other cases.

Chances are, this freaky shit will eventually just stop happening and leave us with a cold case, all dressed up with no place to go. I hope to God. Get anything interesting last night?"

"I bumped into Anders and Ho at the Squeeze Box, and I ran into one of the Lickers at MCs," I said. "Their next match is Saturday night, I've got a few bills down on the Lickers to win, you should join me."

"Uh, yeah. Remind me to ask my wife," he grumbled.

About 11 a.m., Lopez phoned my desk. The Maricopa County Sheriff's Office had contacted him earlier that morning to report that the whole Phoenix Bloody Rollers squad as well as the team which they were hosting out of Flagstaff had gone missing.

"Apparently, Flagstaff derby was due back home early this morning, according to ad hoc associates who reported the team's non-return to police. They remain unaccounted for," Lopez said. "The people in Phoenix have tried to check up on them through the Rollers, but they can't raise anybody on the Roller roster either. And I haven't heard from Veronica or Becca, but I've left them a couple of messages in the past 24 hours."

Denver Day

"They could all just be out partying through a blue Monday though, so it's hard to say for sure what the deal is. I wouldn't rule anything out, but if we never heard from any of them ever again, I wouldn't be surprised. Something else a little weird, too," Lopez went on.

"Investigators out there in the Valley of the Sun said some of the derby circuit people they've been following-up with this morning are reporting that last night was a no-show on the part of both squads, in due course. That the fans showed up to watch the Phoenix-Flagstaff match, but neither team ever arrived to play. On the other hand, some people reported the teams did show up in fact, that the gig went off just fine, that they talked to the girls like business as usual and can report the events of the match in detail."

Wonderful. Schrödinger's cats on wheels. About lunchtime, MacKinney walked over to my desk: "Dispatch just called up here, they have a black-bag call that just came in for this residence," he said, showing me an address on his notepad. It was Anders' apartment.

While I gathered my jacket and hat, the lieutenant sent word through dispatch for the medics to standby upon arrival and, because of the sensitivity of the investigation, to disturb the scene as little as possible. We rolled on the call.

The EMTs were easily able to grant our request not to touch anything or anybody, without violating any obligation of theirs to render first aid, because everyone in Anders' apartment was quite dead. It was obvious at first glance. Anders' body was completely bare, bent over the wooden coffee table. Ho was dead as a mackerel too, seated on the couch in front of the coffee table. Between his and Anders' bodies was a third nude corpse, a female, but different inasmuch as the girl in the middle was furry allover. Furry with fur.

Not only was Ho's dong still inside the wolf lady, but the blade he'd stabbed her with some innumerable times was sticking out of her. She'd bled all over him, all over the couch, and all over Anders who appeared to have been killed by the very sharp teeth of the wolf woman. The moon dog had bitten big fleshy chunks out of Anders, whose body had deep punctures, gouges, and bite wounds from the monster's claws and teeth all over what was left of her ass, legs, and back. She had bled out allover the coffee table and floor.

A few of Ho's errant blade swings at the werewolf looked to have missed its target and snagged Anders' lower body a couple of times as well. His death blows appeared to be the severe and deep cuts and gashes on his neck, made by the evidently very powerful back claws of the hirtuse lady-in-the-middle.

There was a pap of cocaine and blood coating everything in the apartment. The lieutenant lit a stogie, and luckily it didn't touch off the room's funky plume. The tobacco smoke worked to buffer our olfactories from the shimmering madness and maybe had the effect of normalizing the air.

"Take a look at this, Rick," MacKinney said. He lifted the wolflady's ankles with his pen, raising back the fur, under which butterflies were tattooed on the skin of each ankle. Under the lower back fur there was an ivy tramp stamp, on the right wrist a bangle, and under the fur on the nape of its neck was a small barcode tattoo.

"Looks like we've got one of our morgue fugitives back. More or less," he said.

"Guess that's our girl," I said. "Fifty bucks she gets out again."

He shook his head, unwilling to accept the odds. "Dixie's gonna love this. Bag 'em up gentlemen."

We headed to the diner for a late lunch, we both ordered spaghetti and iced tea. We talked about things preferred and quantifiable, like field sports and weather instead of werewolves. After I told him about Lopez's call that morning, the lieutenant unapologetically steered the conversation back to hockey, but I resisted.

"So where are the werewolves in Arizona? Are they the girls who played the match and then disappeared? Or are they the ones who never showed up to play in the first place? Or, are there now two of each team, one wolfy and the other one not so? Maybe there has to be doubling-up of reality before there can be werewolves in the first place." I mused. "If that were the case, then I wonder what the alternate histories are, that lead up to the Chino wolflady and to Dixie's first repeat customer."

"I dunno Rick. Could be that we've got some derelict strain of the lily-white Queen of England who, somewhere in time, is as pure as driven snow. But for our purposes, the queen is iced

Denver Day

down in the Pierce County morgue, covered in jizz, fur, tattoos and I don't know what else."

Better than Going Blind

Friday evening arrived. I worked the phones through dusk picking at the various involved West Coast agencies, debriefing them on the Arizona situation, and telling of our development with Anders, Ho, and Fur Lady #3. No one else (yet) had tracked down any of their morgue skips, neither furrily reanimated ones or otherwise. But the weekend was young.

My desk phone rang about 8:30. It was Lopez again, this time with only a mild doozey. The two San Diego girls who disappeared during the October 11 murder wave, the only ones whose bodies weren't found right there at the scene had just showed up to work at the road house they'd disappeared from after their last shift the previous week.

"The weird thing though Thompson, is that they've lost a week," Lopez said. "They thought they were showing up for their October 10 shift, the one they disappeared after. Their manager let them start their shift, he didn't know how else to react. In fact, he says they're both there now on cocktail duty. So, he phoned me about thirty minutes ago. I'm on my way now to see what kind

Denver Day

of report I can get from them."

"Good luck with that, Lopez. Let's catch up in the morning," I said. When I hung up the phone, the line rang again before I removed my hand. It was Dixie on the other end.

"It's her, Ricky. I did quite a bit of poking around. Her latent canine evolutionary traits have been hyper-accentuated, like she went through some instantaneous evolutionary retrofitting that somehow emphasized certain genes and traits. But, it is her. Or was. There is no doubt about it. A fascinating specimen and unique to my experience."

"She has an elongated jaw, floppy ears, pointy teeth, and a shiny coat but she is, more or less, still biologically very human insofar as her blood work, pH, bone structure, and the like. My previous forensic marks are still visible. However, there's no evidence of any of the embalming chemicals I shoved her with after her previous post-mortem exam. And that's one of the things I can't explain to you in scientific terms. But anyway, I've embalmed her for a second time."

"A couple more things," she paused, rustling papers. "This time, her last supper was the spunky hind flesh of Keri Anders; though her penultimate meal seems to have been a burger and fries, same as Ho and Anders. Maybe she wolferized during intercourse, I really couldn't say. And as to any questions of the when-where-how-why-and-what-the-fuck of her being back from the dead as a wolflady," she paused again, mid-sentence, and shifted the phone to her other ear, "you're just going to have to call a vicar or something. It ain't my department. Anyway, she and the other two are iced down back there. Whenever you have time, you can come have a look if you want."

"I appreciate it Dixie," I said.

"No problem," she answered, and we hung up.

Lopez drove his unmarked sedan down to the topless bar to take statements from the two girls who had lost a week. Down I-5 a few miles, to a nautically themed place called Kat Shakers. The two girls and he sat at a long, wooden table in the manager's office.

They were two very cute, very giggly young Latinas, who reported knowing absolutely nothing about their recent statuses as missing persons. The first they'd heard of the whole story

Denver Day

was when they got to work an hour ago, under the unassuming impression that it was Friday, October 10.

There was very little else for Lopez to include in his report. The girls were genuinely startled at the story they were hearing, but they seemed to look and feel fine. He asked what they remembered about their last 24 hours, and they both recounted the day per their recollection, which consisted of the night of October 9 to the early evening of October 10. They related a seamless and relatively uneventful run-down of events which jive with history, to a point.

Lopez tried to explain to them, best he could, that they had in fact both disappeared under foreboding circumstances, in the early morning nearly a week ago, in the wee hours of October 11, after finishing their shift at Kat Shakers, and that it had been the same morning where dozens of their industry peers were murdered all along the West Coast. He iterated to them that they had been gone just a few hours short of a full calendar week.

"But we just got here," one of them said. They both giggled, sipping sodas. Silly sounding or not, the current date was October 17, and

Lopez suggested they call their friends and family, who must be most assuredly concerned.

Lopez understood that this whole thing was pretty fruity sounding to these women. It was sounding more and more ridiculous to him also. The events he had recently been experiencing while investigating this case and trying to document them, trying not only to put it all in order, but to explain it, to solve it, to close the case were making hay with his understanding of reality, tempting a mockery of his ethical foundations, and turning his work into some kind of weird joke.

And to these two girls, it was just a story; and an incorrect one as far as they understood, as they in fact were sitting right here, living, breathing and cute, visibly antsy to get on with their shifts as cocktail waitresses. It was plain to them. It also was obvious to them that it was obvious to the detective that his story sounded like the screwy one.

Lopez persisted, insisting right back at them that they had been gone for a week. There was no real evidence from the girls' perspective except for words that didn't jive with what they had experienced. Basically, their ears were hearing a weird story, yes, but they were fine. For all they knew, the police and the bar manager were making all of this shit up for some reason.

He told them to let him know if and whenever they remembered anything.

Meanwhile I just rinsed and repeated. I went through the Squeeze Box, which was full of blue smoke and perfumed taint of all sorts. There was nothing of note and I didn't stay too long, although I was almost half-surprised not to see Anders and Ho present in fur. The Diddler was also doing a brisk business, though it felt like there was something missing in the air in there, too. I didn't stay long.

MC's was OK again. I sat and had some nachos, but there was no Alvarez, and no Kitty, and none of my other new weirdo friends. I went by the hotel where Tina's band played, but the band was off that night, for some reason. The relatively quiet jukebox replaced the music source in there for now, and the place was pretty dead.

I drove down to the Lickers' warehouse, where the team was scrimmaging and a good gathering of their groupies were hanging out. It was a typical Lickers' Friday night, and I saw

Sandy and Kitty and waved. They waved back but didn't break formation. None of the bookies were there. I went back to the car, got back on the road. It was raining again.

I drove to the coroners office, and keyed the front door. I walked back to the body lockers and pulled out Anders. There she was, white as a sheet, hard as a rock, stone dead, naked as the day she died. Dixie had cleaned up the blood from the wounds on her running gear. I could see clearly the deep and wide canine-inflicted gouges.

Next I pulled out Ho, whose wounds Dixie had also cleaned, although unlike the teeth wounds on Anders' hind end, Ho's flesh wounds had more of a bunched, shredded lettuce look, since they were inflicted by sharp claws, not sharp teeth.

Next I pulled out the other girl. The furry one. She kind of looked like a bigger version of a puppet alien character from some old television situation comedy. But this was no puppet. She was naked too excepting her shiny fur coat which was a little spattered and matted with dried blood and other fluids. The fur on her underside, her belly and the like, where her eight small breasts were, was much shorter and slicker than the rest

Denver Day

of her coat, though still quite hairy. Some wonder of nature.

I returned the three back to their quiet silos, walked back outside and locked the door behind me. I drove to the diner and read more newspapers over a couple of nice Tabasco omelettes and a pot of decaf. The waitress was chatty and warm, in contrast to the weather. I was there for a few hours during which time the mindful waitress emptied my ashtray multiple times. Mr. Joe de Coffee arrived about 11:30, joining me at the diner bar. He ordered eggs. Dear waitress kept the coffee coming. I filled in Joe about the reinvigorated-come-dead-again furry girl, and of the simultaneous demise of Anders and Ho.

"As of about an hour-and-a-half ago, they were all still at room temperature in the morgue," I said. "But, reality's lately proven fully capable of turning itself upside down, in way short of ninety minutes." I also told him about the other morgue disappearances up and down the interstate.

"You're way more interesting than any newspaper," Joe laughed. He pulled his flask out of his coat, and generously dashed some of its contents into my coffee, then into his own.

Coffeesky. Having finished his own night breakfast, he removed a rumpled pack of smokes out of his shirt pocket and lit one.

"Ricky, this too will pass," he said. "Cheers."

"Yeah. Like a kidney stone," I said. "But yes, cheers."

Denver Day

The Axes Have It

It was now past zero hour. I said my good-nights to Joe and dear waitress, disembarked from the bar stool, and walked out to my car. It was still faithfully drizzling, washing clean the small, new hours of that early weekend.

The radials of the intermittent traffic made a bluish, slickly lubricated glistening sound on the wet street. I started my car, put on the A.M. talk very very low, and let the defrost go to work before I put the engine in gear. The radio played muffled oldies as I motored to my apartment. I stepped out of the car, and glanced up to my front door on the second floor, and there was Kitty, leaning on my apartment door. When I topped the stairs she took one look at me, and said "I'm tired too. Let's go to bed."

"Amen sister," I said. And we did. Saturday morning found us gently awakened by natural tides. The morning was uncharacteristically uninterrupted by phone calls from my ex-wife, or teammates, band mates, beer bashes, or a lover's stealthy flight in the night. Yet. We went at it for about two hours, then had two bowls of generic raisin bran and cold nut milk, each, for breakfast in bed. Or supper, whatever. It was still raining. We went again, shared a smoke, and I asked her who would be tonight's lucky team.

"One of the Seattle outfits. The Plaiden Switches," Kitty said. "They have awesome uniforms, you'll love it."

We both showered up, watched cartoons for another hour, then drove to lunch for pizza. Along with the meal, the eatery offered a live broadcast of a minor league hockey game.

"I love it," I said.

"Me too. A close second to my beloved derby," she said.

My phone rang. Dixie again.

"You want the good news or the bad news first?" she asked.

"Go with the good," I instructed.

"Good news is your three-way victims lasted through the night. They're still here, no funny stuff, still dead as far as I can tell, and two-thirds of them remain furless," she said. "No morphing, no nothing."

"Fantastic, thank you. Good sell. And the backside?" I asked.

"Your sax player's in here too. I'm sorry," she said. "Come on down. And MacKinney said he's hearing some other shit from the other morgues involved with the October 11 cases. I have to admit, I'm starting to tune it out. Anyway, we didn't want to bother you earlier this morning, figuring you deserved to sleep in for once."

"Gracias Dixias. I knew it seemed too quiet. I'll be there directly," I said dutifully.

Kitty smiled at me. "you want to come with me to the morgue?" I asked.

"Allrighty and why not," she said.

We finished our pie and went down to Dixie's cool, dry realm. It still rained, but it wasn't unseasonally cold, and we shook off the damp at the door. Dixie and Kitty exchanged greetings, and we all walked back to the body locker.

"New intern?" Dixie smiled. She rolled Tina out, and pulled back her tarp.

"MacKinney's got the paperwork on this deal. Her bandmates say they had the night off last night. One of them showed up at her place, walked in and found her," Dixie said. "Looks like the tool of record was an ax."

The blow was top down. It looked like a single, well-directed, powerful hit that split through her pan down into her neck like a log longways.

Denver Day

"No sex assault or other such violation. Nothing but the ax. Seems to have been just the one swing."

"Well, there you go Kitty. Forensics in all its glamour," I said.

"Jeez," she purred. "What a mess."

"Thank you Dixie," I said.

"And thank you Ricky," she answered.

I dropped Kitty off at Sandy's apartment, and Sandy plied me with wet, open-mouthed kisses on top of Kitty's many recent ones through my driver side window. She chatted me up for a quick few moments.

"You've been cheatin' on me, Ricky, and I plan to straighten your ass out," Sandy said. "You're due at my apartment after tonight's brouhaha. Do you read me, boy?"

The women grinned at each other goofily.

"Yes, loud and clear. Sounds like a date. And good luck with the Plaiden," I said.

They waved me off, and I made my way to the office, where I found MacKinney at his desk with a few stories for me about the night before.

"I took a statement from the guy who found your late girlfriend. The bass player. He was pretty broken up," the lieutenant said. "He really wasn't able to give me any good leads, names, or suspects, though of course he did mention you. By both his account and yours, she was a solid gal. A former firefighter, a jazz saxophonist and such. A strong woman and genuine lady."

"Yeah. I don't like this at all," I replied. "And no, she doesn't fit the victim profile for this."

"So there's very little else yet, found at the scene and what not. I assigned the case to Smith, since you were so recently intimate with this woman. But brief the detective, and work with him as needed. He's been out pounding the pavement today, and you probably won't see him until Monday. You OK?" he asked.

"I'm fine. I've been kinda swept up with these skater girls in the past few days, and the case too, and I hadn't talked to Tina. But it's hard to say we "drifted apart" because it's been less than a week. There's been barely time for even listing much less drifting."

"Fair enough," the lieutenant said. "In other news, I've heard today from some of the boys up and down I-5, about the October 11 killings in their respective jurisdictions. It seems there were lots of bar fights last night, at the scenes of last week's various crimes. Rather a bit of a blood bath. Various sightings, bashful drunken patrons slightly unwilling to explain to police what they saw. But it sounds like the girls were out last night, haunting the chapel. Furry girls. I fear there's a storm coming, dude."

"Ahhh, the furries," I grumbled.

"Yes, the furries. Rousting about the bars of their initial demise, working on people with the very instruments that were used toward their own ends. Or, at best, just causing near riots because of the hairy bitch-like undead condition their conditions are in," the lieutenant went on.

"For example, the undead fuzzies in Vancouver made hell with the cricket-bat-freeze-block death stick mysteriously procured from the police evidence locker without a hitch. The boys in Seattle and Portland, as you would correctly estimate, have been dealing with buckshot-filled titty bars and barflies, all morning. Longview's bloody hangover today, you guessed it, involves furries loose in nightclubs wearing itchy-hot .357s. Beaverton's dealing with the aftermath of a box-cutter melee, and our lovely neighbor Eugene this morning is more or less one big gaping machete wound. And so on."

"Fantastic. The recidivism should make it easier to find answers," I argued, optimistically. "Relatively quiet here, though?"

"Well, that depends on what you mean by quiet. I would say it's been not entirely silent, in light of the ax murder and the inter-species death tryst involving our suspects," he answered.

Denver Day

Good Clean Fun

Lopez phoned with a somewhat more benign and slightly funnier account of apeshit from San Diego. He said the girls who'd reappeared last night had re-disappeared as they were wrapping up their shift earlier that morning. "Their manager said he'd let me know if they show up again next Friday, or at all," he said.

"Otherwise," he continued, "I'm hearing reports of last night's bananarama from the other jurisdictions. But let the record show that we haven't had any of the furries down here. Not yet anyway. It may be borrowing trouble, but I'd sure be curious to see one of them. All told, it was relatively quiet here last night, compared with the others involved."

"Yes, it's quite a sight, Lopez, and causes a funny kind of feeling in your insides," I glowered. "And I'll be interested to see if it's October 10 yet again, come next Friday down at Kat Shakers."

"Yeh, no kidding. At least they're not getting murdered over and over again, well at least as far as we know, anyway. Call me if you get anything interesting," he said, and we hung up.

As the afternoon came and went west, the

Denver Day

drizzle very temporarily paused. I telephoned Detective Smith. We'd picked him up from the Tacoma city force about a year prior, for slightly better pay and an opportunity to get out from under the traffic hat, though even the lieutenant, not infrequently, finds himself standing at intersections pointing at automobiles in the sleet. To protect and serve. Keep the peace. Stand in the rain. Jumpstart minivans. You tag 'em, you bag 'em. Piss on sparkplugs. So many important duties.

"Heya Smith, Thompson here. How's that coming," I asked.

"It was her own ax that sent her on her way. I've been talking to the band members all afternoon. Tina Santos' most recent party of interest is you. But she had plenty of ongoing boyfriends. Her band mates have given me a few leads on various exes, and I've done some background on them. A couple of art students most recently, a guy and a girl. And some of the band members, over the years, but those occurrences have been rarer, one-night deals, because they've wanted to keep the band intact and functional. I'm paying a visit to the art students next up. Any suggestions?"

"Well, she used to work for the Forest Service, but you probably heard that from MacKinney. Beyond that, she carried herself well and knew how to keep her nose clean. My guesses would be that the killer is some freakazoid who saw her band playing at the hotel, and was there frequently enough to form a fixation," I speculated. "Which may only be once, depending on the freakazoid. If nothing else, I'd say go there and watch the jugs, for starters."

"All right then," he said.

"All right yourself, see you Monday," and we hung up.

About that time, the lieutenant went out the door with his briefcase, off to be with his wife, and promised me he would not be around the office on Sunday come hell or high water. This had been well enough of the office, for a Saturday, to suit my taste as well. If I'm gonna work on the weekends, it's preferably field work, even if it all seems to blend together in the end.

I walked over to the diner for refreshments and a quick rest, before the sun went down and the Lickers went up. I fought off the urge to call Dixie, to see if our people in the morgue were still there. But she wasn't down there this afternoon anyway, and whenever she has something, she always calls me.

After I ate, I drove around the city for a while. I went by the Diddler, and past Tina's band's hotel that was tragically fresh out of sax players. I passed by the Squeeze Box. Both the Diddler's and the Box's parking lots were filling up as the evening heated up.

The Davey Jones Lickers and the Plaiden Switches were set to have at one another at 10 o'clock, though when I got there about 9, the place was already a roiling carnival. I shuffled in and bought some popcorn, grabbing a seat in the bleachers, high enough to get a good, wide perspective all around the track, but low enough to hear some of the skaters' hissing and filthy mouths.

The place was crowded with heavily tattooed people. The motorcycle club demographic had an impressive showing, for example, as did the dark college Bohemes and the chain-smoking high school kids, and a fair distribution of dirt-track shit-kickers. There was a good count of family-night-out examples also.

The concessions were briskly selling, but I did not see any of the bookmakers at the moment. I didn't care about the actual results of my bet, but those bookmakers were relevant to the case, whether they showed up or not. I could see some of the Lickers out through the back doors near where their dressing room was situated. I could see some of the out-of-town team too, in black and white plaid kilts and brown shirts.

The way the old warehouse was retrofitted, both teams had to use the same locker room facilities. I confessed again to myself that the derby was now right up there in my book with ice hockey.

By the time the match began, the place was a complete zoo and it seemed to be already about hip-deep in spilled beer. The Seattle team's fans didn't have too far to travel for this one and their showing was as strong as the locals. The air was shimmery with the event's electricity, and when the composite rubber wheels hit that big lacquered right of way, it sparked the room's energy, which arced throughout the crowd. The noise was loud as hell, and constant. There weren't any combustion engines in the venue but it was just as impressive.

First rolled the Plaiden, shouted out by

Denver Day

some woman on the P.A. Next came the Lickers in blue and gray motley and lace. Both teams were on deck and both fan sets were swinging. It was beyond cacophony.

I saw Kitty and Sandy, and they looked hot. Hell, all of them looked hot and it made the whole place hot and everybody knew it. The whole thing was a giant nascent orgasm, and my mouth watered at all those legs in plaid and motley. Many people did drool if not foam, and the spilled beer in there went from hips-deep to tits-deep in a flash.

Pizza Noir

165

Denver Day

Take it Outside

When the pack got underway, the rubber-on-tracks thunder remained a steady high-decibel minimum threshold for the room. This was a scene for screaming and bullhorns and no kind of candle-lit conversation. The skaters moved with finesse like road-wise truckers working the traffic and their transmissions. I realized quickly the real powerful caliber and potential of these women all balled up and traveling with no fear at high velocity. Each of them were dangerous projectiles.

After a whistle marked the start of the first jam, one of the Plaiden took some sort of blow to the muzzle, but she just toweled off and got back on the track even though she was still dripping a bit. The first bloodied Plaiden didn't deliver her own retribution although a couple of her teammates subsequently hemmed up Sandy, giving her an elbow to the face. As Sandy toweled off her mug, so as not to overlube the track with viscous blood, another Licker took over as the lead jammer.

After this initial quid pro quo activity, the teams' territory seemed properly marked and all off-the-books messages sent, for the time being.

Pizza Noir

The opening elbows had certainly ginned up the crowd. There were a few incidental tumbles during the rest of the first period, but I saw no more head shots connected, at least not until what happened afterward in the parking lot.

I was pretty jazzed up after all the fun of watching the game, like the rest of the crowd. It was a summer-night energy, which made what happened next out in the parking lot all the more surreal and bat-shitty. Everyone was wide awake, but relaxed, and slowly making their way out of the warehouse, finishing their beers and chatting. Tailgating.

As soon as the Lickers and the Plaidens were able to get out of their skates, they were also trickling out into the lot and moving on with their own evenings. Of course I was more or less hellbent to get over to Sandy's. I didn't see her or Kitty, but several of the other skaters had already made their way outside.

There came a commotion at the far side of the parking lot, the end closest to the interstate. I just figured it was a generic parking lot brawl of some sort or another, so at first I didn't bother. But the disturbance continued, and spread, and got louder, and it became pretty clear, pretty

Denver Day

quickly, that it was some kind of organized pack attack, by the way the crowd was moving and responding to action in several locations at once. And then it became clear what exactly comprised the offending pack.

The Chino Wheeled Beavers were there, armed with objects of all kinds, sharp and blunt. And because of their furrified werewolf form, they also had sharp claws and fangs to wield. People were fighting back; some were having success, and some were not. I realized the situation had become one in which I was about to start trying to pick off drowned-zombie wolfladies with my service weapon.

I had 17 rounds on my hip, a couple of extra clips in my coat, and a revolver on my ankle. First I quickly called into dispatch, and told them to roll any available assets toward my location.

"Ricky Thompson here, up off of I-5 at the Davey Jones Lickers' Warehouse. We've got a yard brawl under way out here in the parking lot, and I'm about to have to start picking off members of an armed pack of crazy monsters up here, attacking the crowd in the parking lot," I said.

I refrained from saying "wolf ladies" or "werewolves" over the air. During the few seconds

I was on the phone, one of the things had evidently tried to bugger the wrong tailgater, and I heard a shotgun blast that punctuated the urgency of the situation to the dispatcher at the other end of the line.

"OK Thompson, on our way, give us a few minutes." I heard the emergency tone-out begin over the line before I hung up. At that point, I heard more shotgun and looked up to see its handler. The man was standing on the cab of his pickup truck which was parked right next to a faded and somewhat waterlogged ambulance, which I realized was the Beavers' drowned, undead vehicle.

Somehow these Chino furries had gotten that thing running again, after freeing themselves from the morgue and stealing it back from the Alameda County boys who had fished it (and the Wheeled Beavers themselves) out of the San Francisco bay. Now it was full of buckshot holes, and the furry zombie bitch who the guy had unloaded upon, no longer had a head. But, her hairy body was still running around, bumping into cars and people. Blinded as it was, the thing was not making out well. A crowd of derby fans easily descended on her quickly and violently, dragging her away.

I trotted over to the ambulance and looked inside. I saw no humanoids in there. I scurried up onto the top of the vehicle, pulled out my sidearm, and gave a nod to the dude with the shotgun at my side. He was facing one way, and I faced the other way. He pointed off to my right, and I saw a furry jumping up and down on something, likely somebody. Then I heard someone else unloading behind me, from somewhere out in front of the shotgun guy.

I drew a bead on the jumping furry to my right. It looked like the round struck her square in the back, knocking her forward and down, but she stood back up immediately and turned around to look up at me. She started in my direction with all deliberate speed. I put another round in her front side and it knocked her on her back, but again she got up.

This time she began to charge me, closing the distance quickly. She jumped up onto the top of the ambulance, so I jumped off. The guy behind me removed her head with a shotgun. She fell backwards off the ambulance, stood yet again, headless, but was quickly covered up and hauled off by a vengeful, lusty mass of the living derby fans.

A good stream of vehicles were leaving, but not at the lazy daisy pace at which they'd originally been exiting the event. Nevertheless, quite a few had remained to fight as many others rapidly fled the wicked wheels-off wacky-ass parking-come-nightmare scene. Glorious pandemonium.

I scanned the crowd, trying to find targets, in order to mitigate any of the most serious of things that I could find going on at the moment. The guy with the shotgun had left the top of his pick-up truck and headed into the crowd presumably to do the same thing. It was helpful that the parking lot had thinned out a little, but the area was still a crowded and confused mess.

I could still hear all sorts of mayhem, people screaming, horrifying screams, very probably for legitimately horrifying reasons. I knew that there would probably be a sizable handful of wolverized civilians in addition to various dead wolf ladies after the smoke cleared.

About that time, the first sirens arrived at the parking lot, and I walked up to one of the police units and borrowed his radio, so that all personnel who were on the channel could benefit

Denver Day

from the information I was giving: "There's a guy here with a shotgun, he blew the heads off of two of the furry things, and one of them I'd already shot three of times. So watch out for that, sidearms won't lay them down, at a minimum it takes a head shot with a shotgun.

"Besides myself and the guy with the blunderbuss, there's at least one other person in this crowd who's discharged a weapon, though I didn't see who it was. Basically there are two confirmed furries down, headless, and the crowd dragged off their bodies. I don't have a civilian casualty count, but I have heard the sounds of it."

The incident commander affirmed my traffic, and the officer whose radio I borrowed nodded and went to the trunk of his vehicle to grab his shotgun. EMTs who had just arrived had begun addressing injured.

It was about 11:45. The scene had thinned out further as a steady stream of people cleared out. There were one or two more skirmishes, and by just after midnight, when the smoke cleared, any and all surviving furries were gone.

There were four furry bodies in the parking lot (two of them headless, and the heads of the other two were simply fully bashed in); there may have been more dead furries, but if there were, they were gone now. About two dozen superficially injured people were being tended by medics, and there were three people who had to be transported for more critical medical attention.

We counted seven dead civilians on scene, but it was yet unknown if anyone else, citizen-wise, had been dragged off and was now missing.

Denver Day

One More Saturday Night

We were at the warehouse location until about three in the morning, until all the medical transports cleared the scene, gathering reports or contact information from everyone who had not fled or been killed, and putting a tow on vehicles orphaned by the incident.

This included the Beavers' ambulance, our possession of which I considered to be no less than an invite for monsters to burgle our tow lot. But we had to do something with it, and it's not very protect-and-servey to dump it in the lake.

Of the four re-dead furries known to have not walked away from the parking lot scene, Dixie later said that all of them had been spontaneously gang raped by members of the crowd during the melee, suggesting I'm not sure what all potentially vast sociological and psychological implications, regarding the human condition and pack mentality when besieged by rabid werewolf-women.

We bagged up the four fallen furries and sent them Dixie's way, along with the seven slain non-werewolves (also an act of borrowing trouble in my opinion), along with the wicked ambulance.

Denver Day

On my way to Sandy's, I put in a courtesy call to Dixie.

"Four new horizontal furries coming into your office tonight. And seven new regular stiffs. We are placing a couple of deputies at the coroner's office through the night, and probably indefinitely, until we get clear of all of 'em. Also Dixie, I suggest binding the dead furries with rope. I don't want them loose, two of them still have heads," I reported.

"OK. I'll get my boots and be down to the coroner's office in half an hour," she answered. "Shall I expect you?"

"I'll be in with the sunrise," I answered, "but you be careful. There are still more undead Chino Beaver furries on the loose out there, they're at least smart enough to organize and attack, and seem to know their way around morgues."

"OK. See you in a few hours," she said. "You be careful too, big boy. I know where you're goin'."

We hung up and I set the phone down in my empty passenger seat. The events of the evening had provided me with a sort of plateau moment. The night had initiated some fundamental, permanent dissolution of reality as I'd once thought I'd understood it.

Pizza Noir

This brought to my mind, two points of order. One, it was more of a punctuation event than some shocking revelation, because the "way things were supposed to be" had already long since stopped being "how things are."

And, two, while, yes, this was weird, and, yes, it was unfortunate that there was a significant and heightening body count, it was oddly liberating. In fact, it was good news that as my previous perspective and estimation of the world and how it worked had been identified as incorrect, the result was now that my perception and understanding of the world was now less incorrect, even if only slightly. Even if it was because I knew I could be sure about less and wrong about more.

I pulled into Sandy's apartment lot. It was immediately clear that there was a party going on, and it was a big change in setting and atmosphere. The air was amber with the warm light of tiki torches, and the whole property had a festive, beery atmosphere. It was a far cry from the bluesy, macabre, carnival-like death pall that I'd left hanging over the warehouse lot.

The usual crowd was around the patio bar and courtyard. I moseyed over and a girl back there handed me a lager in a yellow can, lit my cigarette, and gestured toward Sandy's apartment. I thanked her, and headed that way.

Sandy had a bit of a shiner, from the elbow she took during the match with the Plaidens, many if not all of whom were here now, drinking beer and scrumming with the Lickers and their crowd. It looked like the hatchet was fully buried for this night.

Occasionally, Sandy put her cold beer onto her bruised eye and cheek. She smiled at me. Kitty smiled too. A couple of the Plaidens smiled. That one dude who sits in Sandy's flat during parties and plays Sandy's stratocaster, sat again on the smoky couch with some other dude and several other Plaidens. As usual, the record player spun some twangy B-side.

"What's the big idea bringing werewolves to our warehouse!" Sandy ribbed me. Standing in the kitchen, she was arm in arm with one of the Plaidens, and they giggled and nuzzled each other. I realized she was tipsy, and it was the first time I'd ever seen her that way. Both she and her arm candy were drunk like little sailors.

"But seriously. Those girls are following you Ricky. Not us. Watch your back."

Pizza Noir

I don't know exactly what my reasoning was, but anyway this seemed like the wrong setting and wrong crowd for me to explain that I'd been involved in killing at least one of her zombiefied, furriefied circuit peers in the warehouse lot, regardless of whether they were stalking me then or stalking me now or whatever.

Kitty, who was not drunk, chimed in then, "Sandy baby, jeez, he's had a rough night too. Don't give him a hard time. We thought you weren't coming, since you had to stay and work overtime mopping up our parking lot. Glad you finally made it. If you've got blood on your hands, go wash it off. Meanwhile, this is our friend Patchy Plaiden. She's become our opposition favorite. But only since the match ended."

Patchy Plaiden was the tipsy girl who kept making out with Sandy. Kitty and Sandy ordered me and Patchy through the beaded wall, into Sandy's humid, dark and pillowy sleeping quarters. "We'll be in to join naptime after we shut down the party," Sandy said. Patchy yanked at my coat. I figured what the hell, it's been a long night, I'll live a little.

Sunday, October 19. The sound of traffic woke me, though it was still dark in Sandy's sleeper. It was about 9 a.m. I felt around, and there next to me purred Patchy Plaiden, still sleeping like a foxy little log.

Naturally, Sandy was gone. Unusually, Kitty was too. I stood and peeped into the living and kitchenette areas, and there was nobody in there either. It was kind of nice, it had been a crowded bedroom last night, although I and Patchy had gotten the most of each other, and Kitty and Sandy doing whatever they were doing. Everyone had been exhausted and/or drunk, and it had been late, so nothing lasted long but it was nice. Hot and quick then a nice, relaxing and much-needed mid-autumn nap. Patchy popped up, and pulled me back down.

"The girls must've already headed to their day jobs," she said. "You mind driving me up to Renton, detective?"

"No problem, Patchy. And please, call me Ricky," I answered.

"OK Ricky. But first you need to drive me home, again, right in here," she said. She grabbed me with one of her legs, like a skate-fed python. Patchy was awesome.

Denver Day

Costumes

I was rather tardy for Dixie, but she'd understand. Different shifts are different shifts and no one can work all three ceaselessly. I drove the kilted, yawning Patchy up to Renton. Traffic wasn't bad, being that it was Sunday morning. I dropped her off at her apartment. She wrote her number down on the notebook in my glove box and gave me a nice kiss.

I gave her a card, and watched her walk up and key her door before I pulled away. I got to the office of my ex-wife coroner-come-taxidermist about 10:30. Dixie had been there since about four, and she had the four Chino wolf women laid out on tables in the cooler, with their hands and feet bound just in case. The seven regular dead were back there too, in various states of moot disarray. She poured me some coffee.

"I'm about done. Gonna leave those two deputies here and go home to what's left of my weekend. Quite a shit show you boys cooked up last night. What the hell, Rick?"

"Well, basically Dixie, yes there is such a thing as werewolves," I said, looking back at her. But it wasn't like I had to sell that to the woman who'd been dealing with them all week. "I think we're all gonna have to come up with new reasons, for why we ever even bother. All this shit changes things, and particularly so if it doesn't stop. Even if it does stop, the damage to the reality that we once knew, is well done, so it doesn't really matter now what happens. Life as I knew it is over."

"I fully take your point. And if the werewolf-to-slickbodied-corpse ratio remains a rich reality at my office, it begs the question of why I should even bother coming to work anymore. It certainly changes the definition and scope of it, at the very least," she said. "Even if it doesn't stop. Do you think it will?"

"It might. Even if it does, though, I think something else funky will take its place, in some form or another," I answered her. "Normal is a thing of the past."

I looked at the four furry bodies with their hands bound by sheriff's office rope. I looked at the other seven regular stiffs from last night, some of whose faces I met with vague recognition, having seen them in the audience during the match. I walked Dixie to her car.

On our way out we passed the two deputies

with shotguns. They were watching the television in the front of the office, but you could tell they also were quite aware of what they were guarding, or guarding against. All in a day's work.

For some reason, the drizzle had stopped and a foggy blurry sun cooked through the damp air. It was about noon. I drove to the office, the administrative wing of which seemed to be empty but for me. I phoned Wilson at the Oakland P.D. to let him know that we had four of his morgue escapees accounted for in our deep freeze. I left a message with his dispatch, and he phoned back within minutes.

"Black-and-pink miniskirts, black-and-white plaid sports support tank tops, and top-to-bottom furry," I said. "Your girls. Attacked the crowd in the parking lot after a derby match here between Tacoma's Davey Jones Lickers and Seattle's Plaiden Switches."

"We re-killed four of them, two of them had their heads removed by the shotgun of a vigilant derby fan. Seven civilians were killed. This cold crowd is up here at the Pierce County Coroner's office, dead and all trussed-up, under 24-hour armed guard until further notice."

I told Wilson that the rest of the Wheeled

Beavers team were still at large.

"Well, we're glad to be rid of them for now, but of course I wouldn't wish it on anyone. Anyway, I don't think we're truly rid of them," Wilson answered.

"Now we know they can reanimate not just once but multiple times. Mind you, the last time we saw them, they weren't wolfy. Only FirePie Beaver had the shiny new coat. The rest were just dead girls. Of course they all disappeared from our locker days ago, as you know. By the way, do you know if FirePie is one of the ones you bagged?"

"I don't think so," I said. "Going by the uniforms, we apparently nailed Rolling Pinny, Lightning Pelt, Plasma Hat, and The Milkmaid. Let us know if you want them back. Seriously."

"I doubt it. I recommend taking them to your tow lot, dousing 'em with petrol, and having yourselves a bonfire. Probably your safest bet to prevent sequels," he said.

He made a real good point, and the lieutenant, Dixie, and I made it a reality that evening.

"Well, we also ended up with their undead freak-show ambulance. I think we'll torch that too," I said.

"Fine with me," Wilson answered. "Good thinkin'."

I scribbled out a note for Detective Smith, requesting that he update me about the investigation of Tina Santos' murder come Monday, then headed to the diner for decaf and newspapers. The sun hid itself again as I made my way.

I parked, pulled a stool up to the bar, and ordered coffee and eggs. It was a usual Sunday afternoon bustle in there. There was a stack of newspapers on the bar, and I scooted them toward me, fighting off my usual urge to avoid looking at the front page.

Below the fold, a headline read: "Eleven Dead in Davey Jones Lickers Parking Lot Brawl," under which was a color photograph of the Chino Wheeled Beavers' buckshot-dusted ambulance. The copy began as follows:

Tacoma, Wash. (AP)—A rival women's roller derby squad from Chino, Calif., violently attacked fans leaving a match between the Seattle Plaiden Switches and the local Davey Jones Lickers, Saturday night in south Tacoma.

Pizza Noir

Four of the attacking team members and seven bystanders were killed during the incident. The Chino squad were dressed in werewolf costumes, according to the Pierce County Sheriff's Office . . .

"Costumes my ass," I grumbled, putting the paper aside. In came Joe. The waitress brought him a cup, and we sat and chatted with her.

"You get called out to that derby fight last night, Ricky?" she asked.

"Yes and what a mess, ma'am," I answered her. Joe chimed in: "Costumes, huh Rick?" he smiled. Of course he knew differently. Dear waitress smiled and topped off our coffees.

"What are you going to do, Rick?" Joe asked.

"I was talking to Dixie about that just today. For now, I guess, the plan is just to plow ahead, keep showing up at work and keep trying to do my part in the world, whatever that turns out to be. But we're wise to remember, the world spins on its own," I answered him, "and how."

It was getting dark. The waitress topped off our coffee again. Joe whipped out his flask, and dashed whiskey into our cups.

"To costumes," he smiled.

fin comme du gros sel